dish

#7

Recipe for Trouble

friends, cooking, eating, talking, life.

Grosset & Dunlap

dish
#7

Recipe for Trouble

friends, cooking, eating, talking, life.

By Diane Muldrow

Illustrated by Barbara Pollak

Grosset & Dunlap
New York

For Victoria Wortmann—D.M.

Special thanks to
Michelle Fein Morantez, Executive Chef Tom Weaver,
Joseph Fein III, and Jerome Fein of the
Court of Two Sisters, New Orleans, Louisiana.

Text copyright © 2003 by Diane Muldrow. Illustrations copyright © 2003 by Barbara Pollak.
Recipes copyright © 2003 by The Court of Two Sisters. All rights reserved.
Published by Grosset & Dunlap, a division of Penguin Putnam Books for Young Readers,
345 Hudson Street, New York, NY, 10014. GROSSET & DUNLAP is a trademark of Penguin Putnam Inc.
Published simultaneously in Canada. Printed in the U.S.A.

Library of Congress Cataloging-in-Publication Data
Muldrow, Diane.
Recipe for trouble / by Diane Muldrow ; illustrated by Barbara Pollak.
p. cm. — (Dish ; 7)
Summary: While Natasha and Peichi cope with Shawn's growing obsession with cheerleading
and welcome a new girl to their Brooklyn, N.Y., neighborhood, Molly and Amanda
help solve a food-related mystery during a family trip to New Orleans.
Includes recipes for Crawfish Louise, Pasta La Lou, and pecan pie.
[1. Cookery—Fiction. 2. New Orleans (La.)—Fiction. 3. Friendship—Fiction.
4. Twins—Fiction. 5. Mystery and detective stories.]
I. Pollak, Barbara, ill. II. Title. III. Series: Muldrow, Diane. Dish ; .v 7.
PZ7.M8894 Re 2003 [Fic]—dc21 2002154086

ISBN 0-448-42898-9   A B C D E F G H I J

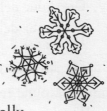

"**S**now!"

"No!"

"Yes—*tons* of snow! Take a look," Molly Moore told her twin sister.

Amanda flung back her sheets and comforter and ran to join Molly on the window seat. She and Molly looked down at the row of small backyards behind the brownstone buildings on their block. The yards had been transformed into a fairyland of glistening white, and the snowflakes were falling with no sign of stopping.

The twins were hit with the same awesome thought. Facing one another, they grinned. "Do you think?" Amanda asked.

Molly quickly checked the windowsill, noting the depth of the fallen snow. She nodded enthusiastically. "Absolutely!"

"Snow day!" they shouted together. The girls giggled. "It's 'the twin thing' again!" Amanda said. That's what the twins called it whenever they said or thought the same thing at the same time.

Molly flopped across her bed and reached for the radio. "...Windsor elementary, middle, and high schools..." The announcer paused. Molly and Amanda drew in tense breaths and waited.

"One-hour delay?" Amanda said hopefully.

"*Two*-hour delay?" Molly was even more optimistic.

"Closed," the announcer finished.

"Closed!" the twins shrieked as they high-fived and jumped around in a circle.

There was a quick rap at the bedroom door and Mrs. Moore came in. She was sleepy-eyed and wrapped in her fleecy robe. "Closed?" she asked.

"Closed!" the girls shouted again, their eyes lit with delight. They jumped around the room, their long brown hair flying in all directions. Without their identifying hairstyles in place—Molly in a high ponytail, Amanda with her hair in the latest style—it would be hard for most people to tell them apart. Hard, but not impossible.

Amanda was more interested in fashion and trends, which was obvious from her bright pink glitter nail polish and her oversized "Princess" nightshirt. Molly, who would rather be comfortable than caught up in the latest styles, had short, bitten fingernails, and was wearing green plaid flannel pajamas that matched her green eyes.

Mrs. Moore realized that the radio announcer had finished reading the lower-school closings and had gone on to the university and college closing information.

She pressed her finger to her lips. "Shhhh, shhhh!" she whispered. The twins grew quiet and listened intently with their mother. Finally the announcer came to the listing they were waiting for.

"Brooklyn College, day and evening classes... canceled."

"Yes!" Mrs. Moore cheered. The twins gave her high fives.

"A day off! Way to go, Mom!" exclaimed Molly. It was fun to see Mom, a college professor, so psyched to have a snow day. Here in Brooklyn, just across the East River from Manhattan, most kids walked to school or took public transportation. The roads had to be really bad—the trains and buses unable to get through—in order for the schools to close.

The twins' seven-year-old brother, Matthew, barged into their room. "Mom, a snow day! Can I go sledding in the park? Would you take me? Could Ben go with us? Please!"

"Who said you have a snow day?" Amanda jumped in.

A puzzled expression spread across Matthew's face. "I heard all the yelling," he said, confused.

"*We* have a snow day, and Mom's off, but *you* have school," Amanda said.

"*Mommm!*" Matthew complained. "That's not fair. Do I have to go? *Please* can I stay home, too? *Pleeeee—*"

"Got ya!" Amanda shouted. "Got ya! Got ya!"

Matthew grabbed Amanda's pillow and threw it at her. "You stink!" he yelled.

Amanda ducked as the pillow sailed over her head and hit Molly. "Hey!" Molly shouted playfully. She pitched the pillow at Matthew, who jumped out of the way. Mr. Moore walked in just in time to catch it.

"Look at these happy faces," he said, his blue eyes twinkling behind his glasses. "It can only mean one thing—a snow day. But I still have to go out there into the blizzard and battle my way to work."

"Sorry, Dad!" the girls sang out together.

"Take the day off," Matthew suggested.

Dad looked out the window and for a second seemed to give the idea serious thought. "I wish I could," he said with a sigh. "But I have a lot of work to get done before we leave." In twelve days, the Moores would be taking a vacation to New Orleans, Louisiana, while Mom attended a conference there for her job. The twins couldn't wait!

"I can't believe spring break is in two weeks and it's snowing this much," Amanda remarked, gazing outside.

"Spring will be here soon," Mom said.

"Well, I'll try to remember that when I'm stuck in a snowdrift somewhere," Dad said. He left the room to get ready for work, not looking at all pleased to have to go out into the storm.

"Can we go to the park, Mom? *Pleeeeease?*" Matthew picked up right where he'd left off.

"All right," Mom agreed. "Let's have some breakfast, and I'll call Ben's mom to see if he can come."

"Hey, Shawn's apartment is up by the park. Maybe she'll want to hang out today," Molly said. Shawn Jordan had been the twins' best friend since elementary school.

"Good idea, Molls," Amanda. "I'll call her right after we eat."

The twins helped Mom make breakfast in the cheerful blue and yellow kitchen. Usually the room was flooded with sunlight from the many windows, but this morning only a murky half-light filtered in, so Mom flicked on the bright overhead lamp. Amanda and Molly made pancakes while Mom made tea and Matthew set the table.

Dad grabbed some pancakes before heading out to work. He slathered each one with raspberry jam and rolled it up. That way, he could eat them with his hands as he rushed off to work. "Mmmm, portable pancakes!" he joked, pulling on his heaviest winter jacket. "Have fun today, you guys. Wish me luck!"

"Good luck!" everyone called after him.

"Come home early," Mom added. "And be careful!"

After breakfast, the twins called Shawn. The phone rang five, six, seven times. The girls looked at each other.

"I guess she's not home," Amanda said. She was about to hang up when the phone clicked.

"Hello?" asked Shawn sleepily.

"Hey Shawn, it's Molly and Amanda!" Molly said. "Did we wake you up?"

"Kind of," Shawn replied. She yawned. "What's up?"

"Oops, sorry about that! Anyway, do you want to hang out today? We have a snow day!"

"I know," Shawn said. "That's why I went back to bed." She yawned again and the twins giggled. "That sounds cool. Do you want to come over? Dad's working on his new book, and it will be totally boring around here." Shawn's dad was a professor at Brooklyn College, just like the twins' mom, so he had a snow day, too.

"Great!" the twins exclaimed. "We'll be over in about half an hour," Molly continued. "See you then!"

The twins hung up and headed to their room to get dressed. Amanda took fifteen minutes to pick out her outfit before she finally decided on a thick teal turtleneck, a fluffy aqua sweater, and her favorite jeans. Molly had put on her comfiest jeans and a cozy gray sweatshirt in no time.

"Come *on*, Amanda," Molly moaned. "You're taking *forever!*"

"I'm almost ready," Amanda said, pinning her hair behind her ears with two sparkly barrettes.

Finally, the family went across the street to pick up

Ben, Matthew's best friend. The two boys were inseparable, partly because Ben's mother, a stay-at-home mom, was Matthew's official babysitter. The Baders had already shoveled their steps, but they were quickly becoming covered with snow again. "Matthew, go up and ring the bell, please," Mom instructed.

Matthew kicked his way through the snow and rang the bell. The door flew open before he had even taken his finger off the bell. Ben was standing in the doorway bundled in a down jacket, snow pants, boots, a cap with earflaps, a scarf, and earmuffs. Mrs. Bader quickly came up behind him. "Thanks for taking him," she called out to Mom. "If he didn't get outside soon, he was going to go nuts!"

Mom laughed. "Kids love snow. I do, too, as long as I don't have to travel in it."

"I know what you mean," Mrs. Bader agreed as she looked up and down the quiet snow-covered street.

"This doesn't even seem like Brooklyn!" Molly said. And she was right. The street was usually full of cars and buses, and the sidewalks full of people hurrying to the subway station.

The five trudged to sprawling Prospect Park, which gave their neighborhood, Park Terrace, its name. Since the snow was still falling, only a few people had started to clear the sidewalks in front of their homes. When the group reached the entrance to the park, the twins said good-bye to Mom and the boys and headed for Shawn's apartment, which faced Prospect Park. "Look—it's Natasha and her dad!" Amanda noticed, pointing toward two people walking in their direction.

Natasha Ross was in the sixth grade at Windsor Middle School with the twins and Shawn and their other close friend, Peichi Cheng. After the five girls had ended up in the same cooking class at Park Terrace Cookware the past summer, they'd started hanging out together and calling themselves the Chef Girls because they all *loved* to cook.

Before taking the class, Molly, Amanda, and Shawn hadn't known Peichi very well. And what they knew of Natasha they didn't like. In fact, in fifth grade Natasha had been the twins' enemy, after she spread a nasty lie that they had cheated on an important science test. The twins didn't know why Natasha was so mean, but Mom had suggested that they forgive and forget. It worked. Natasha started being nicer to the twins in return, and they eventually became friends.

The Chef Girls had formed a cooking club so that they could become better chefs and try new recipes, but soon the club turned into their very own cooking business! They called it Dish, and it was an instant success. There were lots of parents in Park Terrace who came home from work feeling too tired to cook. They loved the fact that Dish delivered delicious home-style meals right to their front doors, meals that included everything from salad and bread to the main course and dessert.

"Hey!" Natasha greeted them.

"Hi," Molly replied. "Hi, Mr. Ross. Did you get a snow day, too?" Amanda nudged her sharply in the side, but Molly didn't understand why.

Mr. Ross smiled. "Well, not exactly," he replied. "Every day has been a snow day for me since last August."

"Um, sorry," mumbled Molly as she felt her face turn red. She'd forgotten that Natasha's father had lost his job as a lawyer last summer.

"That's all right," Mr. Ross assured her. "Really."

"We're going to the Brooklyn Museum of Art," Natasha jumped in. Molly could tell she was trying to change the subject.

"We're heading over to Shawn's," Amanda told her. "Why don't you call us there after you get home from the museum?"

"Can I, Dad?" Natasha asked.

"We'll see," Mr. Ross replied, looking away for a moment.

"It's okay. Shawn's dad is home today, too," Amanda explained, thinking that Mr. Ross would let Natasha go to Shawn's if he knew there was an adult at home.

"We'll see," Mr. Ross repeated. He turned to Natasha. "We'd better get going. It's cold out here!"

They said good-bye and continued on their way.

"Why do I always say such dumb things?" Molly asked her twin.

"That's you, Molls—open mouth, insert foot," Amanda teased. "Seriously, though, don't worry about it. Mr. Ross didn't seem upset. What I want to know is why Natasha's parents are so strict."

Molly shrugged. "That's just how they are, I guess." When they turned into the lobby of Shawn's apartment building, the doorman smiled at the twins and waved them right up.

Shawn was already standing in her doorway when they arrived. *Shawn's looking awesome, as always,* Amanda thought. She and Molly always admired Shawn's cool, confident style. Only Shawn could wear purple cat's eye glasses and make them look totally happening. Today she was wearing black velvet capri pants with a red top. Her curly black hair was pulled back with a red scrunchie.

"Hey!" Shawn greeted the twins. "You two look like you need some hot chocolate. Your noses are all red!"

"It's f-freezing out there!" Amanda said dramatically, pretending to shiver. Everyone cracked up.

"Well, then, today's your lucky day," Shawn replied as the twins started peeling off their scarves, gloves, hats, boots, and jackets. "I made hot chocolate from scratch. I used cocoa powder and sugar, and I even added a drop of peppermint extract!"

"Awesome!" Molly cried, rubbing her freezing fingers.

"*And* we have marshmallows and whipped cream—take your pick!" Shawn exclaimed. She led the twins into the kitchen, where she had set up mugs of her special hot chocolate on the kitchen table.

"This is so good! We should make this for our customers," Amanda said between sips.

"Hopefully, spring will be here soon and we won't have to make them hot drinks," Shawn said cheerfully. "I can't wait for winter to be over. Cheerleading gets really busy in the spring!"

Amanda suddenly lost interest in her hot chocolate.

Shawn had seemed more and more distant to the twins ever since she'd become a cheerleader. And she'd gotten really tight with another cheerleader, Angie Martinez. Angie had to be the rudest, nastiest, most stuck-up person Amanda had ever met.

"*Ooohhh!* I have to show you something Angie gave me," Shawn said, getting up from the table. She hurried into the living room.

Amanda and Molly exchanged worried glances. Molly didn't like Angie any more than Amanda did, although she didn't take Angie's mean behavior quite as personally as her sister did. They followed Shawn into the living room and found her spreading a brochure across the coffee table.

"Isn't this cool?" Shawn asked excitedly. "Cheerleading camp! Angie asked Coach Carson if she knew about any

good camps, and Coach Carson said that
going to camp as a team would help us be
really awesome next year. We'd be there the
entire summer!"

Amanda and Molly looked at each other again. Molly
knew *exactly* what Amanda was thinking: *Cheerleading
camp? Here we go...*

Be cool, Molly told Amanda with her eyes. *Don't make
a scene about it.*

For the next three hours, though, no matter what the
girls talked about, Shawn seemed to bring the conversation
back to cheerleading. The twins hadn't seen Shawn this
excited in a while.

"...And another cool thing about this cheerleading
camp is that the whole team would stay in the same cabin!
It's like going to summer camp with a bunch of friends,
instead of going alone and not knowing anybody there,"
Shawn went on.

"The same cabin? That would be great," Molly said, still
trying to sound enthusiastic.

But Amanda couldn't even pretend to be excited for
Shawn anymore. As she watched the snowflakes fluttering
past the window, she cheered herself up when she remembered that auditions for the spring play were only a week

from Thursday. In the fall, Amanda had had a blast singing and dancing in the school musical, *My Fair Lady*. She felt pretty sure she had a shot at a part in the spring play—Ms. Barlow, who was Windsor Middle School's drama coach and French teacher, said Amanda had done a terrific job in *My Fair Lady*. Just thinking about the spring production made Amanda feel giddy. *I can't wait to be in another play, getting into character, joking with the other kids in the cast. I really hope the audition goes well! Then two days after auditions, we head to New Orleans!*

All of the Moores were excited about their upcoming trip. The twins had never been to New Orleans, but they had spent hours looking at the pictures Mom and Dad had from their honeymoon there fifteen years before. Amanda was especially eager to see the mansions, streetcars, and spooky old cemeteries for which New Orleans was famous.

"I have an idea," Molly said, her voice cutting through Amanda's daydreams. "Natasha might be home from the museum by now. Peichi might be home, too. Why don't we have a conference call with them?"

"Good idea," Shawn agreed. "I can put us on speaker phone and it will be like we're all here together."

Shawn phoned Peichi first, but got the Chengs' answering machine. "She's probably out sledding," Molly guessed.

"Let's try Natasha," Amanda suggested quickly. She didn't want to give Shawn a chance to start talking about cheerleading *again*. When Shawn called, Natasha's mother answered. "Hi, Mrs. Ross," Shawn greeted her. "Is Natasha there?"

"Well...I suppose so," she replied. There was a pause. "I'll get her," Mrs. Ross finally said. "But only for a moment."

When Natasha came to the phone, she spoke in a whisper. "Hi, guys. I can't really talk now. My parents need to talk to me about something important. I'll see you tomorrow in school, okay?" Then the girls heard a soft click. Natasha had hung up.

Shawn looked at Molly and Amanda. "*That* was mysterious."

The twins nodded. First Natasha's dad had acted strange near the park, and now this. What was going on at Natasha's house?

*A*fter Natasha hung up the phone, she returned to the living room and sat down in a wing chair across from her parents. She wondered what this big talk was about. Natasha cleared her throat. "So, what's up?" she asked her parents.

"I have some good news," Mr. Ross began. "You know that since I've been out of work, things have been... well...difficult. But that's all over. I've got a job!"

Natasha immediately relaxed and smiled at her parents. This was wonderful news! She knew how worried they had been about money and the future. Lately, it seemed that that was all they ever talked about. *But now Dad has a job! Things are gonna be so much better around here,* Natasha thought.

"That's great!" she said, her eyes shining happily. "Where will you be working?"

"Well, I'm not exactly sure yet," he answered.

Natasha looked at him, confused. "You have a job, but you're not sure where it is yet? I don't get it."

"I've hired myself!" Mr. Ross said, smiling broadly. "I'm going to open my own business. Start my own law practice!"

"That's so cool, Dad!" Natasha said. "Way to go! You and I both have our own businesses now."

Mr. Ross laughed. "That's right. You have Dish and I'll have the Law Office of T. David Ross, Esquire."

Mrs. Ross cleared her throat. "As you know, Natasha, it takes money to start up a business. Remember how you needed capital when you and the girls started Dish?"

Don't remind me, Natasha thought. Last summer, when the Chef Girls were first talking about starting a business, Mr. Ross had promised them some start-up money. But when he lost his job, Natasha didn't feel comfortable taking the money. Natasha had been embarrassed to admit to her friends that she couldn't help them with the money after all.

"Well," Mrs. Ross went on, "we're going to have to make some changes around here so that your father will be able to start his new law practice."

"What kind of changes?" Natasha asked. She was starting to get nervous.

"When this house was first built in 1893, the fourth floor was designed as the maids' quarters. Later it was converted into a separate apartment—that's why there's a little kitchen up there," Mrs. Ross continued. "And when we moved in, we made the fourth floor part of the regular house."

Natasha nodded. She *loved* the fact that her bedroom was on the fourth floor. Her room was big enough for a large bed, an old wooden trunk, and a chaise. *And* it had an enormous walk-in closet! The year before, Natasha had gotten to pick out the pale purple wallpaper for her room. Sometimes she imagined that she was on her own, living in her own apartment. She looked expectantly at her parents, trying to figure out where they were going with all this.

"Natasha, we'll be turning the top floor back into an apartment, and renting it in order to make extra money," Mr. Ross explained.

"What? What about my bedroom?" Natasha cried. "No! Please don't do that! I love my room! No one will even *want* the fourth floor."

"We've already rented it, sweetheart. A preschool teacher and her niece will be moving in next Sunday."

"Next *Sunday?*" Natasha asked, surprised. *That's so soon!* she thought to herself.

"I know it's sudden," Mrs. Ross said apologetically. "We originally planned to have the new tenant move in next month. That way, we would all have had more time to get used to the idea of renting the fourth floor. But Paula—that's the teacher's name—and her niece, Elizabeth, need to move in right away. You know, Elizabeth will be going to Windsor Middle School. She's in the sixth grade, just like you, so it would be very nice of you if you'd show her around." Mrs. Ross looked like she wanted this conversation *over.*

Natasha couldn't think of anything she wanted to do less than show around this girl who would be taking over her bedroom. "So where do I sleep?" she demanded.

"You'll move to the guest room," her mother answered. "It's really a very nice room, you know."

"It's beige," Natasha countered, "yucky, boring, ugly beige." She took a deep breath and asked, "Can I at least redecorate the guest room?"

Mrs. Ross sighed unhappily. "Not right now. Maybe in a few months, when we won't have as many expenses."

Natasha looked down at the floor. What else could she really do? Making a scene wouldn't change anything—it was obvious that this was a big decision her parents had made without her. *This is totally unfair!* Natasha thought angrily. But then she realized that her dad deserved this new chance. *He's been sad since he lost his old job,* Natasha told herself. *What else can I do besides go along with this?*

"I'll guess I'll start moving my things downstairs," she finally said, rising from the chair. She glanced at her parents as she stood. They were both watching her, looking relieved.

"Here, I'll help," her dad quickly volunteered. "We have some boxes in the basement. I'll go get them."

"Okay," Natasha said as she moved toward the stairs. Mrs. Ross followed Natasha and put her hand on Natasha's shoulder.

"Thank you for understanding, sweetheart," Mrs. Ross said. "It means so much to your father and me. And this isn't permanent, you know. You'll have your room back as soon as things are a little easier financially."

Natasha smiled sadly at her mother, then climbed the stairs up to her beautiful purple bedroom. Once she got to her room, Natasha opened her huge closet and gazed inside. *The best way to start would probably be to pack my clothes,* she thought. But instead, Natasha sat on her bed and looked around her room. It was hard for her to believe that in just a few days, some other girl would be living here—and it wouldn't be her room anymore.

That night at the Moores' house, everyone had just sat down for dinner when Mom made an announcement.

"I have some news," she said. "I received a phone call this afternoon from my department head. It turns out that I need to be at the convention a little earlier than expected—on Thursday instead of Saturday. So we have to go down two days earlier than we'd planned." She smiled. "Two extra days of vacation—isn't that great?"

Everyone stared at Mom with serious expressions.

Amanda gasped. "But then I'll miss the audition!"

"They're not going to be happy about this at work, Barbara" Mr. Moore said.

19

"We're getting our uniforms for softball that Thursday," added Molly.

"And my project on earthworms is due that day," protested Matthew.

"I'm not going," Amanda said firmly. "No way! I am *not* missing auditions for the school play."

Mom stared at them as though she couldn't believe what she was hearing. After a moment, she turned to Dad and spoke softly. "Mike, maybe you've forgotten, but our fifteenth wedding anniversary is that Friday. Going early allows us to celebrate it in the exact same city where we spent our honeymoon."

Dad looked surprised. "Of course I didn't forget!" he said, but the girls had the feeling he wasn't being completely honest. The red flush on his face had given him away. "Yes, you're right. That would be great. I'll work it out."

"As for the rest of you," Mom continued, turning to the kids, "Matthew, you'll have to bring your project in a day early. Molly, the coach will hold on to your uniform until you get back. And Amanda, I'll write a note to Ms. Barlow. Maybe you can audition early."

"No way, Mom!" Amanda protested. "Ms. Barlow will *never* let me do that!"

"How do you know?" Mom asked. "She might."

"No she *won't*," Amanda insisted. "The play is the *only* thing I care about at school. I *can't* miss the audition. I'll

20

skip the trip. I'll stay here in Brooklyn—with Peichi. Or Shawn!"

"Absolutely not, young lady." Mom put down her fork. "You are *not* missing our family vacation. And speaking of the school play, I certainly hope you'll keep your priorities straight and not let it overshadow your schoolwork." Mom looked down at her plate. Amanda swallowed hard.

"Sorry, Mom," Amanda said quietly. "I don't want to miss the trip. It's just that the play is really important to me, too."

"I know, sweetie," Mom smiled at Amanda. "And I'll talk to Ms. Barlow. We'll work something out."

What a relief, Molly thought to herself as everyone continued eating. She was worried that once Amanda was involved in the school play, she might start acting like a star and thinking only of herself, the way she had in the fall. *But Amanda has been trying really hard to be more thoughtful,* Molly thought. *I just hope she keeps it up.*

The next day at school, Amanda rushed through lunch. She wanted to find Ms. Barlow and talk to her about auditioning early for the play. She finished the last bite of her turkey sandwich and gulped down her milk. "Bye, guys," she said. "I've got to go talk to Ms. Barlow. See you after school."

In her backpack, Amanda had the note her mother had written. She had read it over Mom's shoulder the night before.

Dear Ms. Barlow,
    Due to unforeseen circumstances, Amanda must accompany our family on a trip before spring break starts. She is very disappointed about having to miss the audition for the play on Thursday. I'm hoping there might be some way for her to audition at an alternate time. Will this be possible?
    Thank you so much for your help.

Sincerely,
Barbara Moore

Amanda walked down the hall toward room 23, Ms. Barlow's classroom. When she got there, she peeked inside and saw Ms. Barlow sitting at her desk, grading papers. *What if Ms. Barlow says no? What if I can't convince her? It will ruin everything!* Amanda cleared her throat, and Ms. Barlow looked up.

"Oh, *bonjour*, Amanda," Ms. Barlow greeted her. She pressed her hand to her chest. "You startled me!"

Great, Amanda thought. *Not the best way to start things off.* Her mouth felt dry. She cleared her throat again.

"Sorry, Ms. Barlow," Amanda said. "I was—um, I was

hoping I could talk to you about the spring play."

Ms. Barlow brightened. "Oh yes, of course. Come in! Now, the spring play. *Very* exciting, isn't it? I *simply* love *And Then There Was One*. So funny! So suspenseful! Have you read it?"

"Um, no," Amanda replied, feeling dumb. This conversation wasn't going the way she wanted it to. "Actually, I need to talk to you about the audition."

Ms. Barlow looked at her expectantly.

Amanda took a deep breath and said, all in a rush, "My family is going on vacation for spring break and we're leaving early. We were going to leave on Saturday but we just found out last night that we have to leave on Thursday instead, so I would have to miss the auditions, but I really, *really* don't want to! I want to be in the spring play more than anything, and I was hoping—that—that there would be some way I could audition early." She placed her mother's note on Ms. Barlow's desk. "I brought a note from my mom," she finished lamely.

Ms. Barlow read the note quickly, then looked thoughtfully at the ceiling. Amanda bit her lip and thought, *Will Ms. Barlow think I'm asking for special favors? Will she think it's bad that I'm leaving school before the break officially starts?*

Finally, Ms. Barlow looked back at Amanda. "Normally, I like everyone to audition in the same way, at the same time," she began. "It's *completely* fair that way.

23

But I would *hate* for you to miss the audition when it's clearly *so* important to you! Let's see...I think we can do something for you!" she continued. "You can perform a monologue for me the day before the regular auditions. It will be just like a professional theater audition! You know what a monologue is, don't you?"

Amanda was pretty sure that a monologue was a long speech in a play where an actor spoke at length without being interrupted by another character. But she didn't want to let on that she didn't know for certain.

"Absolutely," Amanda told Ms. Barlow. "I'll be there with a monologue. Thank you *so* much."

Ms. Barlow smiled. "You're welcome. I'll see you next Wednesday after school. *Au revoir.*"

"*Au revoir,*" Amanda sang back happily. She hurried down the hall, turned a corner, and stopped to lean against a wall. "Yes!" she cheered in a whisper. That had gone better than she ever would have dreamed—now she would have her very own private audition with Ms. Barlow!

Now all I have to do is find a monologue, Amanda thought. *And memorize it. In a week!* She gulped. Amanda suddenly realized that the special audition would be harder than the regular one. *Leaving early on this trip is making everything complicated!* she thought with a sigh.

chapter 3

After school, Natasha was surprised to find her normally quiet house full of workmen stomping around. Her father stood on the second-floor landing, talking to a man in jeans, a flannel work shirt, and a heavy vest.

"Hi, sweetheart," her father called to her with a wave. "I'll be right with you. I'm a little busy. Your mother had to go out."

Natasha said hello to her father, then started to climb the stairs to the fourth floor. The sound of the footsteps was heavier up there and she could hear other noises, too—hammering, an electric drill, a radio playing hard rock. A workman on his way downstairs brushed past her. More heavy footsteps banged above her. Suddenly, Natasha had a terrible thought. *Are the workmen in my room? What about all of my stuff?* The night before, Natasha and her parents had started packing her belongings, but they hadn't finished. *Who said these people could just go into my room and mess with my things?*

Natasha raced up to her room. She gasped. Everything was gone—her bed, her dresser, her clothes, her stereo! Everything! All that was left was the soft, fluffy rug covered in roses. All the doors on the fourth floor had been taken off their hinges, and several workmen were painting the hallway, bathroom, spare room, and kitchen. The fourth floor already looked like a different place.

Heading back downstairs, Natasha ducked out of the way of two workmen who were carrying a brand-new refrigerator. She ran to the guest room and found all of her belongings crammed into the smaller room. Natasha could barely squeeze past the chaise to reach her bed! On the floor were five cardboard boxes with Natasha's books, CDs, and pictures. Her journal—Natasha's most important possession—had fallen out of one of the boxes and was lying on the floor, in plain sight. Blinking back tears of frustration and anger, Natasha thought *I hate this room! It's so ugly! How could they just go through my stuff and stick me in this awful, tiny room?*

She ran downstairs to find her father. "Dad!" she demanded. "It's such a disaster upstairs! All my furniture and stuff is taking up the entire room. *Please*—I can't stay in the guest room. I hate it!"

Her dad looked uncomfortable. "I know it's a bit of a squeeze in there—we'll figure it out later. Mom and I thought the workmen would just be painting the fourth floor today, but they have another job and can't come back tomorrow to move your furniture. We don't have much time before—"

"Where's Mom?" Natasha interrupted.

"She'll be right back," her father replied. "She went for her manicure."

The word "manicure" stopped Natasha cold. Had her mother really gone off to get a manicure? How could she spend money on her nails when the whole family was supposed to be making sacrifices? *Mom made me give up my room—but she can just go off and get a manicure? That is so unfair!*

"This is too much!" Natasha angrily told her father. "I'm stuck with this tiny, disgusting, ugly room that I can't even redecorate, while *she's* out getting a manicure?" She grabbed her jacket from the hall closet and yanked open the front door.

"Wait, Natasha," her father called.

"No! I'm going over to Molly and Amanda's. I'll be home before dinner," she called over her shoulder, then slammed the door behind her. With her head bent down to shield her face from the wind, she ran toward the Moores' house. Natasha sort of hoped that she would run into her mother on her way home from the nail salon. She was in the mood to confront her mom right then and there, and she didn't care *who* might see them.

Panting, Natasha knocked on the Moores' front door. Amanda swung open the door, looking a little puzzled to see her.

"Hey Natasha!" Amanda said. "Come in."

"I just thought I'd come by," Natasha said. "Is that okay? I'm sorry I didn't call first."

"No, that's fine. Come on up," Amanda said as Natasha hung up her coat. The girls went up to the twins' bedroom, where Amanda's bed was covered with paperback books of famous plays and computer printouts. "I'm looking for a monologue," Amanda explained. "Ms. Barlow is letting me audition for the play next Wednesday before we leave for New Orleans."

"What monologue are you going to do?" Natasha asked.

"I don't know!" Amanda wailed. "I can't decide. I thought of doing Juliet's speech on the balcony from *Romeo and Juliet*. But that's a lot harder than you'd think. Maybe you can help me pick one."

Natasha sat on the edge of Molly's bed. "I'll try."

Amanda picked up a script and was about to start reading it when she noticed Natasha's sad expression. Amanda realized she was doing it again—thinking only of herself. Her New Year's resolution had been to be more considerate and less self-centered. Right now she wasn't exactly living up to it. *Ugh,* Amanda thought. *I brought Natasha up here so I could ask her what's going on, and I immediately started talking about myself!*

"No, forget it," Amanda said, putting down the script.

"What's happening with you? You seem upset."

"I guess I am," Natasha admitted. "My parents are being *totally—*"

Just then, Molly burst into the room, waving a royal blue shirt. "I got my uniform!" she cried. "The coach got them early, so she handed them out at practice today!" She laid the shirt and matching pants out on the bed. "What do you think?"

"It's nice," Natasha agreed.

"Natasha was about to tell me something that's bothering her," Amanda said quickly.

"Oh, sorry," Molly said. "What's up?"

Natasha explained everything that had happened, and Amanda and Molly listened sympathetically. "It's gonna be so weird! I don't want to live in a *boarding house!* I can't stand the thought of strangers there all the time." She sighed. "So that's that. I'm out of my room for good, and total strangers are moving into my house."

"That's rotten, Natasha! But you're gonna have to find a way to make the guest room work out," said Molly. "Is there any furniture that you can keep in the basement or something? So your room's less crowded?"

"Molly! How can you be so—practical when Natasha's in the middle of a crisis!" Amanda said. "She wants sympathy, not advice!"

Natasha had to smile. "Actually, I was looking for both," she told the twins.

WINDSOR
WARRIORS

"Well, I think it's *terrible!*" Amanda said. "Just terrible."

"Oh, I agree!" Molly exclaimed. "It's *definitely* not fair. But you *do* have to make the best of it. Once parents make a decision, they usually stick with it. Hey, I have an idea! Amanda and I can help you decorate your room!"

"Mom says there's no money for redecorating," Natasha told them, looking down at her hands. "The guest room—I mean my room—has to stay the same boring beige it is right now."

"No, it doesn't," Molly disagreed. "We can help make the room all yours. Posters don't cost a lot. And you could probably save some money from Dish and buy some purple paint! Shawn and Peichi are good at all that stuff, too. They'll help."

"If Shawn's not too busy cheerleading," Amanda said, rolling her eyes. Molly poked her sister's arm. "Okay, okay. I know she'll help. She's the artistic one."

Molly reached over and patted Natasha's arm. "Don't worry! We'll help you fix up your new room. You'll love it!" For the first time since Natasha had heard the news, she smiled at the twins.

"Hey, would you two listen to me read some of this monologue?" Amanda requested. Now that Natasha's problem seemed resolved—at least for now—she felt more comfortable getting back to her own dilemma.

Before they could answer, Mom's voice buzzed over

the intercom. "Girls?" she called. "Is Natasha here?"

Molly buzzed her back. "Yeah, why?"

"Natasha, your mother is on the phone. She's been looking for you everywhere."

Natasha slowly stood up. "I *told* my father I was coming over here," she said, rolling her eyes. She reached for the cordless phone. "Hello, Mom?...Yeah...But I told—bul—no. *Don't* come pick me up. I'll come home right now." She covered the phone with her hand. "Would you guys walk me home?" she whispered.

"Of course," Molly told her. Amanda went to tell Mom they were going to walk Natasha home as Natasha quickly hung up with her mother.

Downstairs, the three girls bundled up and stepped out into the gray, dying light of the late afternoon. They walked up Tall Street and then turned on Natasha's block. Before long, they were at her front steps.

"Thanks, guys. Wish me luck," Natasha said, making a funny face at the twins.

"Good luck," the twins chorused.

Amanda and Molly waved, then turned and walked back home. Natasha watched them go and thought about how nice it must be to have a brother or sister, especially a twin. No matter what happened, you never had to face things alone.

Mrs. Ross opened the front door before Natasha was even halfway up the steps. "You are in big trouble, young lady," she began. "How dare you just go out like that without leaving me a note! I was frantic—I didn't even know if you'd made it home from school! You *know* better. Don't you ever—"

"Wait a minute," Natasha replied. "First of all, I told Dad where I was going. It's not my fault that he forgot to tell you. Did you even ask him?"

"He wasn't here when I got home."

Natasha glanced at the shiny pale pink polish glistening on her mother's nails. "Then you should be mad at Dad, not me," Natasha said angrily. "*He's* the one who forgot to write you a note. You embarrassed me in front of Amanda and Molly and their mother. I didn't do anything wrong!"

"You're right," Mrs. Ross said softly. "I'm sorry. I was just so worried about you."

Natasha blinked hard. She was expecting her mother to *argue* with her, not *agree* with her. After a moment Natasha spoke more softly. "I just wish you'd asked my opinion before you let new people move in here."

"This is something we *had* to do," Mrs. Ross explained gently. "Believe me, Natasha, I'd rather not have tenants move in, either. But you know Daddy and I wouldn't let just *anyone* come live here. We interviewed the new tenant and she's very nice. And I'm sure her niece is, too. Who knows, it could be fun for you to have someone your age living here. It might be like having a sister."

Natasha pictured Amanda and Molly walking together on the snowy sidewalk and something inside her softened. "Maybe," she said.

"They're from the Midwest, from Minnesota," Mrs. Ross continued. "Really, it won't be so bad. Imagine how difficult it will be for *them*, moving to a different part of the country, not knowing anyone."

"I suppose," Natasha agreed. Suddenly she felt tired. She sighed. "Mom, I'm sorry you were worried. I figured Dad would tell you that I went over to Molly and Amanda's for a little while."

"Thank you, Natasha." her mother said softly. She leaned over and gave Natasha a quick kiss on the cheek. "Your father and I appreciate your cooperation. I know it's not easy for you to give up your room. Daddy and I want to do whatever we can to make it easier for you. We'll figure out which furniture to move to the basement so the room is less crowded. And I can help you start unpacking right now, if you'd like."

"Thanks, Mom," Natasha replied. "Is it okay if I use the computer first?"

"Sure. But I'd like you to start your homework before dinner, okay?"

"Okay." Natasha went to the computer, which sat on a table in the den. She logged on and e-mailed the other Chef Girls.

To: happyface, qtpie490, mooretimes2
From: BrooklynNatasha
Re: Just a thought

Hello Chef Girls,

I was talking 2 my mom and she told me that the new people who will be living with us are from the Midwest. They don't know anyone here. I was thinking we could welcome them by cooking some Midwestern dishes this Sunday. What special dishes do people eat out there? Does anybody know?

Anyway, let me know what you think. See u guys 2morrow @ school.

N.

chapter 4

On Sunday morning, Mrs. Ross introduced Natasha to their new tenants, Paula and Elizabeth Derring. Elizabeth was so petite that she made Natasha feel like an absolute giant. Wavy auburn hair framed Elizabeth's face, and her dark blue eyes twinkled as she bounded up to Natasha. "Hey," Elizabeth said. "It's nice to meet you. I love your sweater!"

Natasha smiled, looking down at her fuzzy purple pullover.

"Elizabeth *loves* purple," the woman standing by the living room window said, laughing. She was Elizabeth's aunt Paula. Unlike Elizabeth, she was very tall, and she had short dark brown hair. Natasha could see that they were related, though, because they had the same intensely blue eyes.

"I guess we both like purple," Natasha said, trying not to feel envious of Elizabeth for getting the room that she herself loved so much. Natasha pushed the thought out of her mind. "Don't get anything for dinner," she said. "My friends and I have a cooking business, and we'd like to make you a 'welcome to Brooklyn' meal."

"Well, thanks!" Aunt Paula said, looking impressed. "That sounds great."

Mr. Ross came into the room. "Here are keys for the front door and for your apartment," he said.

"I'm going to the Moores' to cook. I'll be back by five-thirty," Natasha told her mother. She turned to Elizabeth. "If you need any help unpacking, I'm free tonight. And I can show you around school tomorrow if you want."

"Thanks," Elizabeth replied with a warm smile. "That would be awesome."

At the Moores', the Chef Girls sat around the big kitchen table planning what to cook for the Rosses' new tenants.

"What do they eat in the Midwest?" Peichi asked. She giggled. "Probably not sushi or wraps!"

"They probably eat the same stuff we eat," Shawn said as she paged through the Dish cookbook the girls had put together. It contained all the recipes they'd cooked since they had started Dish last summer. "But I bet they have, like, local specialties we haven't made."

"What about sauerkraut and pickled herring?" Molly asked. "I think that's popular in the Midwest."

"What is pickled herring?" Shawn asked. "Isn't herring a kind of fish?"

"They turn a fish into a pickle?" cried Matthew as he walked into the kitchen carrying the Moores' fat tiger cat, Kitty. "That's gross!"

"They don't turn it into a pickle!" Molly announced in her best big-sister voice. "They *pickle* it."

"But what is pickling?" Amanda asked. "How do you pickle something?"

"I don't have a clue," admitted Molly.

"How's it going?" asked Mom, who followed Matthew into the kitchen.

"Mom, what do people eat in the Midwest?" Amanda asked.

Mrs. Moore thought for a moment. "My college roommate was from the Midwest. She made a great casserole that had layers of scalloped pota- toes and pork chops, with sauerkraut on top. I have the recipe if you want it."

"Sauerkraut!" Molly cheered. "I knew it!"

The girls looked at the recipe. "We don't have some of this stuff," Amanda said. She looked at Mom. "Mom, would you—"

"No problem!" Mrs. Moore interrupted her. "I need to go to Choice Foods, anyway."

During the drive to the supermarket, Molly wrote down their shopping list. "We need pork chops and sauer- kraut," she said. "We need something to drink. Apple cider would be good. We can make a green salad, too, so we need lettuce, cucumbers, and tomatoes. Should we make something for breakfast tomorrow?"

"Definitely," Shawn agreed. "We could make some of our great blueberry muffins."

"And brownies for dessert!" Amanda said.

The girls used money they'd earned from previous cooking jobs to pay for the groceries. When they returned from the store, Amanda and Peichi began to peel, slice, and layer the potatoes in a large casserole dish.

"Put salt, pepper, and a dab of butter between each layer of potatoes," Mom told them. "Then you season the pork chops and fry them in a pan with onions and oil." When the chops were done, Amanda and Peichi took them from the pan and poured water into it. The little bits of onion and meat that were left over floated to the top. The girls poured the mixture over the potatoes, then layered the chops on top. "The sauerkraut goes on top of that," Mom instructed. "Cover it and let it bake for about forty-five minutes."

"While that's cooking, let's make the brownies," Shawn suggested.

"Good idea," Natasha said. "Peichi and I can make the salad."

"I'll make the muffins," Amanda volunteered.

"Applesauce!" Molly exclaimed "We have some apples and cinnamon. I *love* applesauce with pork chops!"

By five o'clock the meal was prepared, wrapped, and

ready to go. "*Mmm*, this smells great!" Peichi said with a big smile.

"Want a ride?" Mom offered.

"That's okay. It's not even dark yet," Molly replied. "But we'll call you when we're ready to come home."

"All right. Have fun," Mom said as they walked out the door.

When they arrived at the Rosses', the Chet Girls carried the food up to the fourth-floor apartment. Elizabeth opened the door.

"Dinner's here!" Natasha announced. "Elizabeth, this is Molly and Amanda Moore, Shawn Jordan, and Peichi Cheng. Chef Girls, this is Elizabeth Derring."

Everyone said hello, and Elizabeth led the girls into the living room, where she introduced them to Aunt Paula.

"This is so wonderful of you," she said. "Look at all this delicious food!"

"We're not really unpacked yet," Elizabeth said, gesturing at the many cardboard boxes.

Aunt Paula opened one box and dug out a lace tablecloth. She tossed it over the top of another box. "But that doesn't mean we can't eat in style," she said.

"We thought you might not be unpacked," Molly said, pulling paper plates, cups, and utensils from a bag. "Actually, our mom thought of it."

The girls took out the food containers. When Aunt Paula and Elizabeth saw the casserole, their eyes lit up.

"Hot dish!" they cheered together.

"Hot *what?*" Amanda asked, confused.

"You've never heard that expression?" Aunt Paula asked. The Chef Girls shook their heads. "It's what we call this kind of dish. What would you call it?"

"A casserole," Amanda said. "But 'hot dish' sounds better!"

"Have you girls eaten yet?" Aunt Paula asked. "If you haven't, please join us. There's so much food here."

"Okay," Molly said. They all sat down to eat.

"This is just wonderful," Aunt Paula raved after her first bite. "You girls are wonderful cooks!"

Elizabeth's mouth was full of food, but she nodded enthusiastically.

"Tell me, how do you like Windsor Middle School?" Aunt Paula asked.

"We love it!" Shawn said. "They have an awesome cheerleading squad."

"You're a cheerleader?" Elizabeth cried excitedly. Shawn nodded. "Me, too! I tried out for Coach Carson last week and she's gonna let me join the squad midyear."

Great, Amanda thought, *another cheerleader.*

"Cool!" Shawn said. "You'll love the girls on the squad. They're really fun, especially Angie Martinez."

"What else do you like about the school?" Aunt Paula asked.

"We have an awesome drama club," Amanda said.

"I'm auditioning for the spring play on Wednesday. I'm all stressed out, though, because I still have to find a monologue!"

Aunt Paula got up and opened the top of a box marked "Books." After a little digging, she came up with a pale green script. "This is a script for the play *Broadway Dreams*." She flipped through the pages until she found what she was looking for, and handed the script to Amanda. "Try this one. Read the part of Olivia."

"You know about monologues?" Amanda asked, surprised.

"Aunt Paula used to act in college," Elizabeth said. "She knows, like, *everything* about plays. That's so cool that you're an actress, Amanda. I would never be able to act! I'm *really* bad!" She dissolved into giggles.

"Amanda, why don't you give the monologue a read after dinner? We can give you feedback," Aunt Paula offered.

After dinner, Amanda read the monologue out loud. It was about a young actress' dreams of stardom. Amanda could easily relate to the character's feelings. *This is perfect!* she thought. Everyone clapped when she was done.

A little later, Molly checked her watch. "We'd better get going," she said. "I'll call my mom for a ride. It was great to meet you! See you at school tomorrow, Elizabeth!"

"Bye!" chorused the rest of the girls as they followed Molly downstairs. Natasha was the last one to leave.

"Natasha?" Elizabeth asked. "After everybody goes home, would you help me pick something out for school tomorrow? I don't have a clue what kids in Brooklyn wear!"

"No problem," Natasha told her reassuringly.

Maybe it's not going to be so bad having people live here, she thought to herself.

On Wednesday after school, Amanda hurried to Ms. Barlow's classroom to perform her monologue. Ms. Barlow was already there, waiting for her.

"Begin whenever you're ready," Ms. Barlow said warmly, gesturing to the small stage in the front of the classroom.

Here goes nothing, thought Amanda. Her hands shook as she stepped up to the little stage.

She took a deep breath and began Olivia's monologue.

"...Dreams? Yeah, I've got dreams. I wanna get out of this small town. Make an audience laugh—and cry. See my mother in the fifth row, proud that I finally made it on Broadway—"

Amanda blanked. The silence of the big classroom seemed to swallow her.

She groped for a line—any line.

"'Proud that I became—'" prompted Ms. Barlow. She

smiled at Amanda. "I can't help myself, I know that role by heart! Carry on!"

"...proud that I became somebody, ya know?" said Amanda, blushing as she finished the line.

Luckily, the rest of the monologue came easily, though Amanda felt as if she couldn't breathe throughout the whole thing.

When she finished, Amanda took a deep breath and looked out at Ms. Barlow, who seemed to be deep in thought. Amanda studied her face for clues.

"Well, that was it," Amanda said nervously.

Ms. Barlow looked up at her. "Interesting approach," she said. "Thank you, Amanda."

"Interesting approach?" What does that mean? Amanda wondered.

"When will you assign the parts?" Amanda asked as she put on her coat.

"I'll post the list on the Monday after spring break," Ms. Barlow said as she crossed the room, her high heels clicking on the linoleum floor. "Now I've got to run and pick up little Morgan at the babysitter's. Have a wonderful vacation, Amanda! See you in two weeks!"

How will I ever wait that long! Amanda asked herself. *The suspense is killing me already!* Amanda pulled on her backpack and called good-bye after Ms. Barlow as she flew out the door.

Meanwhile, in the gym, cheerleading practice was about to begin. The squad was warming up, waiting for Coach Carson to come out of her office. Shawn and Elizabeth were stretching their legs.

"Shawn! Girlfriend! What's up?" yelled Angie Martinez from across the gym. She hurried over to Shawn, her long blond hair swinging behind her. Angie's brown eyes flicked once over Elizabeth, but she quickly turned her back on her so that she was talking to only Shawn. Angie cracked her gum loudly. "Am I late again? Did I miss anything?"

"Nope," Shawn replied. "Angie, this is Elizabeth. She just moved here from Minnesota and she's joining the team."

"Yeah. Hi," said Angie abruptly, then turned back to Shawn. Angie opened her mouth to speak, but Coach Carson had entered the gym and girls were lining up in front of her.

"Ladies, sorry I'm late. We've got a lot to do today, so let's get working! First I want to introduce Elizabeth Derring, the newest member of the squad. This is her third day at Windsor Middle School, and I know you'll all make her welcome." She paused as the girls waved to Elizabeth. "Now, let's get into position. You all know the routines weren't tight enough last week. So show me how much better you can be! Let's go!" As the girls ran onto the gym floor, Coach Carson called out, "Elizabeth, stand next to Shawn and try to follow along. Don't worry if you can't keep up yet. You'll get it after a few tries."

But once the music from the coach's portable stereo flooded the room, it became clear to everyone that Elizabeth didn't even need a few tries. Elizabeth made cheering look effortless—her motions were sharp and precise, and she moved across the gym floor gracefully. *Everyone* noticed, and everyone was impressed.

"That was great, ladies!" Coach Carson yelled as the music died down. "Elizabeth! Wow! How long have you been cheering?"

"Just this year," Elizabeth said, beaming. "But I've been doing gymnastics since I was three."

"Really? Can you do tumbles?" Coach Carson asked, her eyes excited.

"Sure," Elizabeth said casually.

"Well, let's see some," Coach Carson instructed. The girls made space for Elizabeth on the gym floor. Elizabeth took a deep breath with her hands at her sides. She paused a moment, and then did five perfect back handsprings across the gym floor.

"Wow!" shouted the team. Several girls ran over to congratulate Elizabeth. Shawn was one of them.

Angie was *not*.

After practice, Coach Carson asked Elizabeth to stay after practice for a few minutes. So Shawn changed back into her school clothes and walked home with Angie, who was practically silent. Shawn was pretty quiet, too. She always felt tired after a long day of school and a hard workout at practice.

"Elizabeth was awesome out there, wasn't she?" Shawn finally said.

Angie let out a sharp laugh. "*What?* Girl, she was a total spaz. You probably couldn't tell because she was right next to you. But every time she moved, she jerked around. It looked *way* bad. Coach should stick her in the back, where people won't see her."

Shawn didn't reply. From the way Coach Carson had been raving about Elizabeth's moves, Shawn didn't think there was much chance that Elizabeth would be put in the back row. Shawn was glad their walk was almost over. She decided to change the subject.

"Hey, wouldn't it be cool if we had a cheerleader sleepover during spring break? What do you think? I might ask my dad if we could have it at my apartment."

Angie looked off into the distance. "Yeah, good idea," she said curtly. "Anyway, see you tomorrow." With that, she turned onto her street.

Shawn watched Angie's tall figure walking down the street. Dusk was falling, and Shawn was eager to get home and have dinner with her dad. She shook her head and walked the last two blocks to her apartment, wondering what made Angie get in such a bad mood sometimes. Sometimes Molly and Amanda—especially Amanda—could be a little moody, but their moods were never as, well, *dark* as Angie's. *I'll call Molly and Amanda when I get home. I can't believe they're leaving tomorrow morning!* Shawn thought.

When Shawn got home, the apartment was dark and quiet. *Dad's not home yet,* she thought. *I wonder why.* Then she noticed the light blinking on the answering machine. She hit the button to listen to the message.

"Hey, baby girl, it's Dad. My faculty meeting was rescheduled for later today, so I probably won't be home until seven-thirty or so. Have a snack and we'll figure out dinner later. Love you."

Beep.

Shawn sighed. She hated it when her dad had to work late. Ever since her mom had died a few years before of a long illness, it had been just the two of them. Now that Shawn was eleven, her dad let her stay home alone, but she didn't like being all alone in the empty apartment. It wasn't that she was scared, exactly—she was lonely. She picked up the phone and dialed the twins' phone number. After three rings, Amanda picked up.

"Hello?" Amanda asked breathlessly.

"Hey, Manda, it's Shawn." Shawn felt better just hearing Amanda's voice.

"Molls, pick up! It's Shawn," Amanda called. Then she turned back to the receiver. "What's up, Shawn? We're packing. Our room is a *disaster!*" She started to giggle.

"Actually, *Amanda's* side of the room is a disaster,"

Molly's voice broke in. "She must think we're going to New Orleans for, like, two *years* instead of less than two *weeks!* She's packing *everything* she owns!"

"No I'm not!" Amanda retorted, laughing. "Shawn, talk to Molly. Maybe she'll listen to *you.* She only wants to bring two pairs of jeans and four tops! That's not enough, right, Shawn?" The twins cracked up, and Shawn laughed, too.

"Well, Molls, I think Amanda has a point," Shawn said. "But I guess you could always borrow some of her clothes if she's bringing so much stuff."

"Yeah, I think we all know that's *exactly* what's going to happen," Amanda cracked. Just then, Shawn heard Mrs. Moore in the background.

"Girls, this place is a mess. Have you packed *anything* yet?" Normally Mrs. Moore sounded calm and collected, but now she sounded frazzled.

"Sort of!" the twins yelled together. Amanda turned back to the phone. "Shawn, we gotta go. Our mom will flip out if we don't finish packing soon. She wants everybody to go to bed early tonight. We have to leave really early tomorrow morning!"

"Oh, okay," Shawn said. "I just wanted to tell you guys to have a great trip. I can't wait to hear all about it when you get back."

"Thanks!" Molly said.

"Have a good spring break!" Amanda added. Still giggling, the twins hung up.

Shawn silently hung up the phone, and turned to face the quiet apartment. Suddenly she missed the twins so much it felt like they had already left.

chapter 5

"Molly! Amanda! Wake up! We have to get a move on!" yelled Mrs. Moore from outside the twins' door.

"I'm up! I'm up!" Amanda called cheerfully. Molly yawned and burrowed deeper under her thick, puffy comforter.

"Molly! Get up!" cried Amanda, pouncing on her sister's bed and tossing her covers on the floor. "Aren't you excited?"

"Yeah...but not at five o'clock in the morning," Molly said with a yawn.

"Don't worry, you can sleep on the plane," Amanda told her.

Molly rolled her eyes. "Ugh! How can you be so cheerful in the morning?" She slowly got out of bed and threw on a pair of sweat pants, a Windsor Warriors softball T-shirt, and a green sweatshirt. Molly glanced at Amanda

"Amanda, it's a plane ride, not a fashion show," Molly said, looking at her sister's outfit. Amanda had put on her light blue top with the lace sleeves and a royal blue miniskirt, and was pulling on a pair of suede boots. "And you won't be comfortable on the plane."

50

But Amanda was busy with the curling iron and didn't answer her.

When both twins were ready, they went down to the kitchen for breakfast. Matthew had his head on the table. He looked too tired to eat his cornflakes.

"Hurry up and eat your cereal, kids," Mr. Moore directed as he gulped a cup of coffee. "The car service will be here in fifteen minutes." The twins sat down and Molly reached for the milk. That moment, they heard a loud car horn out front.

"The car's here already!" cried Mom in dismay. Molly and Amanda raced upstairs for their suitcases.

"Girls! Let's go!" shouted Dad from the landing as the car honked again.

"We're coming!" the twins sounded in unison.

Finally everyone was piled into the car, with their luggage in the trunk. The sky overhead was gray and gloomy.

"At least we'll probably beat the traffic," mumbled Dad sleepily. He leaned back and closed his eyes.

But he was wrong. The traffic was heavy, and the car crawled along the expressway. Mom grew more and more anxious. "We should have left earlier," she murmured, tapping her foot rapidly.

After what seemed like forever, the Moores got to the airport. Molly, Amanda, and Matthew clambered out of the car, glad to stretch their legs before getting on the plane.

"Stay close to me, kids," Dad called as Mom went to the ticket counter. After waiting in a long line, Mom finally rushed back to the family.

"The flight leaves in twenty minutes and they've already started boarding, but I think we'll make it. Let's hurry!" she said, and the Moores took off running down the hall toward their gate. They didn't stop until they reached the metal detectors. Mom walked through briskly, followed by Matthew, who was now completely awake—and super-hyper. Then Dad went, followed closely by Molly and Amanda. But as soon as Amanda walked through the detector, a shrill alarm stopped her in her tracks. *Beep! Beep! Beep!* She jumped back in surprise. A sullen-looking guard approached her and said, "Empty your pockets into this tray, miss." He handed Amanda a small basket. She quickly dumped in a handful of change and some Kleenex, then went through the metal detector again.

Beep! Beep! Beep!

Amanda felt her face grow hot as she started blushing. *This is soooo embarrassing!* she thought. She could hear the people behind her growing impatient.

"This is ridiculous. We're going to miss our flight!" a man grumbled. Amanda looked straight ahead, pretending she hadn't heard anything.

"Take off all your jewelry and your belt," the guard instructed, and held the tray out again. Blushing fiercely, Amanda took off her rings, watch, bracelet, earrings and belt.

"And the hair clips," the guard said  impatiently. Amanda practically ripped them out of her hair. She tried to stay calm as she walked through the metal detector again.

Beep! Beep! Beep!

"Come over here, miss," the guard said, gesturing to a row of chairs behind the X-ray machine. Amanda looked helplessly at Mom.

"Go ahead, sweetie," Mom called.

The guard took a hand-held metal detector and swept it in front of Amanda, then behind her. When it was near Amanda's boots, it made a noise.

"Take off your boots and socks, miss," the guard told Amanda. With a sigh, she sat down and took off her boots and socks, her fingers fumbling with nervousness. She stood up, barefoot. One guard examined her boots, while another sent her through the metal detector again. She held her breath as she walked through, expecting to hear the piercing *Beep! Beep! Beep!* again. But this time, there was just—silence.

Phew, Amanda thought.

"A lot of the time, it's the boots," said the guard with a smile as he handed them back to Amanda. "There can be steel in the toes." Amanda put them on as quickly as she could and stuffed her jewelry, hair clips, and belt in her backpack.

"Great. Now let's go!" Dad said. The family ran to the flight gate and made it just in time. Mom made sure the kids' seat belts were fastened. The jet started moving down the runway, and Amanda grabbed Molly's arm excitedly.

"Here we go!" said Molly as the jet's engines rumbled and the plane suddenly lifted into the air.

The flight was smooth, and by the time the Moores landed in New Orleans, they had forgotten about the morning's travel hassles.

"Cool," Amanda said as their taxi pulled up to the curb in front of their hotel, a modern highrise. Dad went to the check-in counter with the twins, while Mom took Matthew to find the bathroom.

"Hello. I'm Mike Moore," Dad said to the woman behind the desk. "We have a reservation for two rooms here."

The woman typed into the computer and frowned. "I'm sorry, sir, but there is no reservation for Mike Moore here."

"Maybe it's under my wife's name—try Barbara Moore."

The woman typed into the computer again. "No—there's no reservation under Moore. And the hotel is completely booked, I'm afraid. There's a big education conference in town."

"And my wife is here for that conference!" said Dad. "May I please speak with your supervisor?" The woman disappeared into a back room and soon returned with a man in a suit and tie.

"Mr. Moore, I am terribly sorry for this misunder-standing," the man said smoothly, extending his hand. "Please accept our apologies. There are two rooms available at an equally comfortable hotel on Saint Charles Avenue, if you're interested."

"All right. Thanks," Dad said with a sigh. Mom and Matthew arrived at the counter and learned about the change in plans.

"I'm so relieved there are rooms available at the other hotel," Mom said, as everyone went outside and waited as Dad hailed a taxi.

"Is there a pool at the new hotel?" Matthew asked. "Or an arcade room?"

"We'll see, sport," Dad said, ruffling his hair. Matthew ducked out of his reach.

"I'm so *hungry*," he whined. "When are we going to *eat?*"

The Moores stared out the windows as the taxi made its way to the hotel.

"Look! A train!" Matthew called out, pointing.

"That's not a train, young man, that's a streetcar," the taxi driver corrected him. "What you see is the Saint Charles Line, the oldest continuously operating streetcar line in the world! You folks should take a ride while you're in town—you'll pass the oldest part of the city and see grand mansions from the 1700s, historic monuments, Loyola and Tulane universities, and a great zoo, the Audubon Zoological Gardens." He pulled over. "Here we are—Rivet Mansion."

Amanda and Molly stared up at a huge old mansion.

"*Ohmigosh*," Amanda whispered.

"*This* is our hotel?" Molly asked in disbelief.

"Yes, it is, young lady," the driver said as he stepped out of the taxi to take their luggage from the trunk.

"It's awesome. So huge! So...fancy!" Amanda raved as she gazed at the wide wraparound porch, many small balconies, and decorative wrought-iron railings.

"Enjoy your stay in New Orleans," the driver said, getting back into the taxi.

"Thanks," Mom replied.

The Moores went up the front stairs and stepped into an elegant entrance hall. A deep red plush carpet led them to a marble-topped front desk.

Behind the desk stood the most magnificent woman the twins had ever seen. Her jet-black hair was piled high on her head and held in place with a set of carved ebony hairpins with tiny glittering gems. Her dress, made of a gauzy lavender material, flowed around her as she walked out from behind the desk to greet the Moores. Ornate, jeweled rings sparkled on her fingers.

"Welcome!" said the woman in an elegant accent. "I am Madame Rivet, proprietress of Rivet Mansion.

Enchanté, enchanté." When she saw Matthew, she bent down and whispered loudly, "That means, 'I am delighted to meet you,' young man!"

Matthew, for once, was speechless as he stared at dramatic Madame Rivet, fascinated by the one wide silver-gray streak in her gleaming hair.

She looks like someone out of a play, thought Amanda.

Mrs. Moore quickly replied, "*Enchanté,* Madame Rivet. I'm Barbara Moore. This is my husband Mike, and our children Molly, Amanda, and Matthew. Thank you so much for finding us accommodations on such short notice!"

"*Avec plaisir!* It is my pleasure," Madame Rivet said. She handed Mom two brass keys. "You are in rooms one-oh-six and one-oh-seven in the west wing, which I trust will be to your liking. Dinner will be served in the dining room at seven this evening." Madame Rivet rang a small silver bell that sat on the marble desktop, and a young man in a red-and-gold uniform appeared. "The porter will show you to your rooms." As he started to load their suitcases onto a brass trolley, Madame Rivet snapped open a lavender lace parasol and held it over her head. "*À bientôt,*" she called as she stepped out the front door and strolled onto the porch. "See you soon!"

"She is *way* cool!" Amanda said.

Mom nodded, smiling. "Let's go see our rooms."

The porter showed them to a sweeping staircase that led to the second floor.

Amanda turned to Molly. "Wouldn't it be cool to wear, like, a really fancy ball gown with a hoop skirt, and walk down this staircase on the way to a ball?" she asked excitedly. "It would be just like *Gone With the Wind!*"

"R-i-i-i-ght," Molly answered skeptically.

"Actually," the porter interjected, "There *is* a ballroom on the first floor. It's past the library, on the other side of the parlor. All of the rooms on the first floor are open to guests, so you're welcome to take a look at it later, if you'd like.

"Here we are," said the porter as they arrived at rooms 106 and 107. "I'll bring up your luggage shortly."

Mr. Moore gave the porter a tip and he disappeared down the staircase. Mrs. Moore opened room 106 with one of the brass keys Madame Rivet had given her.

"Well, I guess this room is for the twins," she said, looking in.

"*Wow*," whispered the girls at the same time. "This room is *unbelievable!*" Amanda added. And it was. The room had smooth oak panels on the lower part of the walls, with mint-green silk wallpaper above the paneling. The two big windows were framed by rich green velvet drapes, and the oak twin beds had elaborate canopies of the same material. On the wall was an oil painting of a beautiful young woman, and a small chandelier with crystal pendants sparkled from the ceiling.

"It sure is," Mom said with her loud laugh. "This place is lovely! I'm so glad the other hotel lost our reservation." She glanced at her watch. "It's already almost six o'clock. Let's get washed up and unpacked, and then we can head downstairs for dinner at seven." As Mom, Dad, and Matthew went next door to room 107, the twins could hear Matthew's voice.

"Why do they get their own room?" he whined. "No fair! I want my own room, too!"

Molly shut the door, and it closed with a soft *click*. She turned to her sister, her eyes shining brightly.

"Manda," she said, "this trip is going to be *awesome!*"

"There's only one table here," Amanda whispered to Molly that night as the Moores entered the dining room. "Where do we sit?" The long table had been set with elegant china for many people, and some of the other guests were already seated.

"Come, join us," an attractive young woman with black hair called to the Moores.

Amanda felt a little nervous about sitting with people she didn't know. Molly looked over her shoulder to see what Mom would do.

"They must serve the meals family style," Mom said,

looking at the one long table. She took the lead and sat down at one of the empty spots.

"Hello," said the young woman who had waved to them. "I'm Isabelle Rivet. Welcome to my family's hotel."

"Wow!" Matthew exclaimed. "You live here? Neat!"

Amanda elbowed her brother. *Matthew!* she whispered. Isabelle seemed really cool, and here was Matthew embarrassing them in front of her. But Isabelle just laughed.

"Actually, not anymore," Isabelle explained. "I'm in college now, so I'm just home for spring break. But I did grow up here."

"How fascinating," Mom said, smiling at Isabelle. "Where do you go to school?"

While her mother and Isabelle chatted, Molly looked around at the other guests. Across from her were two middle-aged couples who smiled at her. An elderly man and woman joined them, and so did a family with a girl who looked about five years old. At seven o'clock exactly, a clock in the lobby chimed. As if on cue, Madame Rivet entered the room grandly. She seated herself at the empty seat at the head of the table. *Bon appétit!* she said.

Immediately, waitresses and waiters streamed into the dining room, carrying bowls and platters of food that they placed on the table. "This looks great," Dad said, serving himself a helping of spicy catfish and following

it up with seasoned rice and black-eyed peas.

The mother of the little girl spoke to him. "Each night the meal is more delicious than the night before," she said.

Amanda wanted to talk to Isabelle, to ask her about the history of the hotel, the city, and college. But Isabelle and Mom kept talking about colleges and Isabelle's classes for most of the meal.

Toward the end of dinner, Madame Rivet rose from the table. "For the benefit of our new guests, I just want to remind everyone that breakfast is served in this room promptly at eight o'clock. You are all welcome to explore the hotel and gardens, but I must insist that you refrain from entering the east wing of the hotel."

Amanda and Molly exchanged excited glances. What was Madame Rivel hiding in the forbidden east wing?

chapter **6**

*T*hunk!

"*Owww!*"

"*Shhhhhhh!*" Amanda hissed.

"Sorry," Molly whispered, picking up the delicate antique chair that she had accidentally knocked over. The twins were in the dimly lit parlor of Rivet Mansion, exploring the beautiful rooms on the first floor. Mom had wanted them to go to bed early, but they were both *way* too excited to fall asleep, so they decided to check out the hotel. Since the twins had their own room, it had been easy for them to sneak downstairs.

"Okay, the porter said that the ballroom was on the other side of the parlor," Amanda said, looking at the double doors on one side of the room. "So it should be right through there."

"Who cares about the ballroom?" Molly said. "We can check it out tomorrow. *I* think we should find the east wing! This might be the only time we can explore it without tons of people around! Who knows what Madame Rivet has hidden in there? She could have tons of jewels or—or—voodoo stuff or something! Or maybe it's haunted!"

Amanda turned to face her twin. "No way, Molls," she said firmly. "We can't go to the east wing, remember? That's one of the rules. What if we get caught and our whole family gets kicked out of the hotel?" She flung open the double doors and groped around for a light. When she found the switch and turned the lights on, even Molly forgot about the east wing for a while.

"*Wow!*" Amanda breathed. They had found the ballroom! It was a large, open room with high ceilings and a polished parquet floor. The walls were draped with creamy silk wallpaper with a design of tiny gold roses. In one corner of the room was a baby grand piano, near the big bay windows that stretched from floor to ceiling and overlooked a beautiful garden. It was the most elegant room the twins had ever seen.

While Amanda was fascinated by the gorgeous ballroom, Molly soon became bored and wanted to keep exploring. One side of the ballroom had several doors, and one by one, Molly opened them.

"Hey, Manda? This door is to the library, I guess. I'll be in here," she called out.

"*Mmm-hmmm,*" Amanda murmured, picturing herself in a fancy ball gown, dancing in the lovely room.

After a few minutes, though, Amanda was ready to see the library. She walked through the door Molly had found, and found herself in a large, paneled library with red leather wing chairs and hundreds of books. A small lamp glowed on an end table next to one of the chairs.

"Molly?" Amanda called softly. "Molly?"

There was no answer.

"Come on, Molls, where are you? This isn't funny," Amanda said a little louder as a chill ran up her spine. She took a tentative step forward and called Molly again.

Suddenly Amanda felt someone grab her arm! She shrieked, then instantly clamped her hands over her mouth.

"Relax, Manda, it's only me!" Molly whispered excitedly. "Come here—you have *got* to check this out! There's, like, a secret door back here! This part of the book-case opens—it's so cool!"

Amanda followed Molly to the bookcase, and sure enough, she saw a dark passageway on the other side of the shelves. Amanda clutched Molly's hand.

"Come on, let's go in," Molly whispered.

Amanda held back. "I don't want to," she answered. "It's spooky."

"No it's not," Molly countered. "I was in here before you started shouting for me. It's just like a hallway. Come on, Manda! How many times in your life will you actually have the chance to explore a secret passage?"

"Okay," Amanda reluctantly gave in. "But only for a few minutes."

Once their eyes had adjusted to the dim light, the twins

noticed a spiral staircase at one end of the passageway. With their hands on the rail, they carefully climbed the stairs. At the top, they found another hallway.

Amanda grabbed Molly's shoulder. "Listen! Voices!" she gasped. Her fingers tightened on Molly's shoulder. "This place *is* haunted!"

Molly listened hard to the murmurs. She leaned her head against one wall. "I don't think these are ghosts," she said. "These are real voices."

Amanda put her head against the wall. She almost thought she could hear the laugh track for a TV show. She put her finger to her lips, gesturing to Molly to be quiet. The twins moved farther down the hallway, still listening at the wall. "I want to go see Amanda and Molly," a voice said. "How come they get their own room?" Now *that* was a voice that both twins knew well—their brother Matthew.

"They're probably sound asleep, and you should be, too." It was Mom!

"We're on the other side of our rooms!" Molly exclaimed. "We're behind the wall of the room where Mom, Dad, and Matthew are staying."

"Mom! Dad!" Matthew cried. "I heard talking in the walls. This is a haunted hotel!"

Molly and Amanda clapped their hands over their mouths and looked at each other with laughter in their eyes.

"We'd better get out of here before we get caught!" Amanda whispered, dragging Molly through the hallway and down the staircase, back to the library. It wasn't easy for them, since they were rushing in the dark, but they made sure to close the trick door embedded in the bookcase. Once they were past the ballroom and out of the parlor, Molly and Amanda raced back to their room.

The moment they reached the second floor they met Mom and Matthew standing in the hall. Matthew stared at the twins with wide eyes. "*Busted!*" he whispered.

"Where have you two been?" Mom asked, looking sternly at the twins.

"We just wanted to see some of the hotel," Molly answered as she tried to catch her breath.

"We have a big day tomorrow. Get some sleep," Mom ordered as she opened the door to the twins' room and led them inside.

"Guess what! The hotel is haunted!" Matthew told them. "I heard ghosts talking in the wall!"

"Cool, what were they saying?" Amanda asked, trying to keep a straight face.

"Amanda! Don't scare him. You know there are no ghosts," Mom scolded.

"I don't know, Mom," Molly said, winking at Amanda. "This place is over two hundred years old. An old mansion like this would be a good place for a ghost to live."

"They're just teasing," Mom assured Matthew.

Amanda suddenly clutched her head. Matthew grabbed Mom. "A ghost has her!" he shouted.

"My barrette!" Amanda cried. "I dropped it somewhere. Oh, no!"

The twins exchanged worried glances. If Madame Rivet found it in the secret hallway, she would know that they had been there.

"We'd better go back to look for it," Molly suggested.

"You can find the clip in the morning," Mom said firmly. "I know how exciting it is to be here, but we have a very big day tomorrow and it won't be as much fun if you're all tired! It's bedtime—right now."

Molly and Amanda both knew that when Mom used that tone, there was no use arguing. They would have to look for the barrette in the morning—and hope that Madame Rivet wouldn't find it before they did.

chapter 7

On Friday morning, their parents' anniversary, the twins went to their mom and dad's room before breakfast. Mom was sitting on the bed, working on her laptop computer. "Morning, girls," she said with a smile.

"Hi, Mom. Happy anniversary!" Molly gave Mom a hug. "Can we check our e-mail when you're done?"

"Thanks, sweetie! I just need a few more minutes with the computer." As soon as Mom was finished with the laptop, she handed it over to the twins.

"Cool! We already have an e-mail!" Amanda exclaimed.

To: mooretimes2
From: happyface
Re: miss you M&A!!!

Hey Molly and Amanda! I miss you guys! How is your trip? I bet it is awesome!!! ☺ Shawn is having her big cheerleader sleepover tomorrow night so the cheerleading team can get 2 know Elizabeth. Wish her luck! Shawn

68

invited me and Natasha but we said we
understood that it was a cheerleaders-
only thing. I think she didn't want
us 2 feel left out, which was nice,
especially since Natasha and Elizabeth
live in the same house. Anyway, Omar
IM'd me last night 2 tell me about
this movie thing that is tomorrow
night, too. I don't know, I guess a
bunch of people R going or something,
it sounds like fun, so I just said,
"Hey, sure, I'll go!" So I'm gonna go
2 that movie instead of the sleepover.
E-me if you get a chance! I can't wait
2 hear all about your trip. Are you
taking lots of pictures?!?!?! G2G!!!
Love, Peichi

"Peichi writes just like she talks!" Molly said, giggling.

"Does Omar usually IM Peichi?" Amanda asked, puzzled.

"She never mentioned it before."

"*Hmm*," Amanda said. "Should we write her back now?" She glanced at the clock. "Madame Rivet said we had to be at breakfast at eight o'clock sharp and it's almost eight now."

Mom looked over at the clock, too, frowning slightly.

"Dad had better hurry up," she said. "Otherwise we *will* be late! And we have a big day planned."

Just then, Dad came out of the bathroom dressed and ready, so everyone went down to the dining room.

"What is this big day about, anyway?" Molly asked. But Mom and Dad just smiled at each other.

"You'll have to wait and see, kiddo," Dad said to Molly. "It's a surprise!"

Then Molly noticed something that made her forget about the big surprise. She grabbed Amanda's arm and pulled her off to the side. "Manda, look!" she whispered, pointing at one of the place settings. Amanda's sparkly blue barrette lay next to a glass. "Did you drop your barrette at dinner last night?"

"No way," Amanda shook her head. "I *definitely* had it after dinner. Whoever found the clip remembered that that's where I sat at dinner! They know I was exploring the secret passage!"

Just as she had the night before, Madame Rivet entered the room, followed by waiters and waitresses carrying tureens of oatmeal and platters stacked high with pancakes. The twins exchanged worried glances. Who knew they had been in the secret passage? And more important—would he or she tell Madame Rivet?

After breakfast, the Moores left the hotel. Parked in front was a tour bus with a big green alligator painted on it. Day-Glo green letters on he side of the bus announced "Swampland Adventures." Mom and Dad walked toward the bus, and the twins turned to each other. *Swampland Adventures?* they wondered.

"Is that an amusement park? Cool!" exclaimed Mallhew.

"Well, it's not an amusement park, exactly," Mrs. Moore said as she helped him up the steps of the bus. "But we will be riding a boat!" Though Matthew kept pestering Mom and Dad for more information, they refused to say another word about where they were going.

After picking up a few more passengers from other hotels, the bus left the city for a more rural area. The bus driver picked up a microphone.

"Welcome, everyone, welcome to Swampland Adventures. We should be reaching Cypress Swamp in about an hour, depending on the traffic around the great city of New Orleans here. Speaking of, are y'all enjoying your visit?" The passengers chorused yes.

"Good! I love this city and I know that y'all will, too. Now, who can tell me what New Orleans's nickname is?" The twins looked at each other. They didn't have a clue.

A man in the back of the bus called out, "The Big Easy?"

"Yes, sir, that's one nickname. Life here is so nice, we

call living here the big easy! There's another nickname, too—the Crescent City, on account of the mighty Mississippi River that curves around in the shape of a crescent. And it's thanks to the Mississippi that we even have this city. This area used to be underwater, beneath the Gulf of Mexico, but after millions of years the Mississippi left enough silt on the gulf bottom that this whole area eventually became swampland. But the river and the gulf are always in a tug-of-war, so to speak. The center part of New Orleans is actually five to ten feet below sea level— it's basically shaped like a dish, which means that New Orleans is always in danger of flooding."

Molly turned to Amanda. "That's really crazy," she said.

"Yeah," replied Amanda. "This is like school, but better!"

The driver continued telling the passengers all sorts of interesting facts about New Orleans, and after about an hour, the bus pulled up in front of a small building that had a "Swampland Adventures" sign just like the bus. Three men wearing jeans and Swampland Adventures T-shirts came over to the bus, and split up the passengers into three small groups. A tanned man with shiny black hair greeted the Moores.

"Welcome to Cypress Swamp!" he exclaimed in a loud, friendly voice. "My name is Captain René. Are you ready to get on the boat?"

A few feet from the building, three small motorized boats floated in murky water. The boats had open sides, with canvas awnings on top to protect the passengers from the sun. One by one, the Moores carefully boarded one of the boats, followed by Captain René. Once everyone was settled, Captain René started the motor, and they were off, gliding through the still water. The swamp was very peaceful and green, with tall, stately cypress trees draped with thick moss that clung to their trunks and hung off the branches. As Captain René piloted the boat, he told the passengers a little bit about himself.

"My name is René Benoit, and I have lived in the Louisiana swamps for my entire life. I'm Cajun, which you might have guessed from the way I speak. Cajuns are descendants of the Acadian people from Acadia, Canada, who were exiled in the 1750s because of their religious beliefs. As the Acadians settled in Louisiana and married people of other nationalities, the Cajun people were formed. The name Cajun comes from 'Acadian'—if you say it fast, you can hear how much the words sound alike. The Cajun people have lived in harmony with the swamps and bayous of southeastern Louisiana for generations. Over the years, we Cajuns have developed our own culture. We have our own language, our own *fais do-do* parties, and our own delicious cuisine."

"Dodo parties?" Matthew repeated, cracking up.

Captain René grinned. "Not *dodo* parties, *fais do-do* parties! *Fais do-do* means 'go to sleep' in French—these parties last late into the night, so *les enfants* are put

73

to bed right at the party while their parents dance!"

By this time, the boat was deep into the swamp, with no signs of civilization. Captain René cut the engine, and the boat drifted silently through the water. The sounds of many different birds and strange chirping bugs were the only noises in the still, heavy air—until Matthew suddenly shouted.

"Look! Look! It's an alligator!" he yelled, pointing at what looked like a bumpy floating log—with eyeballs! In his excitement, Matthew leaned over the side of the boat and started to lose his balance.

"Be careful, Matthew!" Mom exclaimed, yanking his shirt to pull him back onto the bench. Captain René laughed at Matthew's enthusiasm.

"Yes, the swamps are full of alligators, so don't fall overboard!" he joked as the alligator swam lazily toward the boat. Mom kept a firm grip on Matthew's shoulder as the twins peered at the alligator. "Alligators can stay underwater for three hours," Captain René went on. "And look out for their jaws—when they bite, they can have ten thousand pounds per inch of force!"

"Whoa," Matthew said, looking impressed.

"Hey, *bébé.* Hey, *cher,*" Captain René called softly to the alligator as it approached the boat. Captain René turned to the passengers, who were watching him with wide eyes. "I take three tours out almost every day," Captain René explained. "All the alligators in this swamp know my voice—we are practically friends!"

Mom leaned over to Molly and Amanda. "Those are French words he's using," she told them. "*Bébé* means 'baby' and *cher* means 'dear.'"

Captain René started up the engine and piloted the boat around a bend in the river. He pointed out a simple wooden shack built on the bank of the swamp.

"Does anybody live there?" Molly blurted. *I totally can't imagine living out here with no people around,* she thought. *It's so different from Brooklyn!*

"Not there, no," Captain René explained. "That house was part of a set for a movie that was filmed here. But I will tell you that my house looks a lot like that one, but sturdier!"

"It's a movie set?" exclaimed Amanda. "Awesome!"

"You live in a *swamp?*" Matthew asked. "That is super-cool!"

"What's that bird called?" Mom asked, pointing to a long-legged creature that fluttered gracefully from a cypress tree to rest in the water.

"That's a heron," said Captain René. "Amazing birds! They catch fish for their dinner by placing a small floating object, like a feather, on the water. When the fish surfaces to take the bait, *snap!* The heron catches the fish!"

He pointed out several other animals as the boat

glided leisurely along the bayou, including otters, beavers, hawks, and a funny-looking rodent called a nutria that somewhat resembled a beaver. "The nutria is not native to the swamps," Captain René told the passengers. "They were brought here from South America originally. Nutrias are big pests—they eat too many plants, and make the marsh disappear. There are hundreds of different plants in the swamp, and each one is vital. The Spanish moss you see hanging from the trees has traditionally been very important to the swamp ecology. It makes a good home for many creatures—birds, bats, and snakes."

"*Bats* and *snakes?*" Amanda asked, a panicked look spreading over her face.

"The Cajuns used the moss for many things—clothing, animal feed, caulking for their cabins, medicines," continued Captain René. "It has even been used to stuff mattresses and automobile seats! So, you see, it is a very important, very valuable plant."

Captain René piloted the boat into a dark area of the swamp, where the thick trees blocked the sunlight overhead, and the air was damp and chilly. The twins shivered and Amanda pulled her pale green sweater around her shoulders. The peaceful swamp seemed different here—spookier, more sinister. Captain René spoke in a voice so low that everyone had to lean forward to hear him.

"There is a legend about the swamps," he began, looking very serious. "There is a swamp creature—a swamp beast—called the Roux-Ga-Roux. Whatever you do in the swamps, you must stay away from the Roux-Ga-Roux!" He paused, and Amanda shivered again.

"Why?" Matthew asked in a quiet voice, his eyes wide.

Captain René lowered his voice again. "Because the Roux-Ga-Roux roams the swamps, looking for—anyone. And if the Roux-Ga-Roux finds you, you'll never be seen again...because then *you* become the Roux-Ga-Roux!"

"*Cool*," Matthew whispered. The twins moved farther into the center of the boat. Captain René flashed his dazzling grin.

"But don't worry, *mes amis*," he said. "We haven't lost a tourist yet!" Captain René started the engine and piloted the boat back into the brighter part of the swamp. Soon, the Swampland Adventures building could be seen in the distance, and the Moores knew the tour was almost over.

"There is one more thing you must see before you leave Cypress Swamp," Captain René announced. He opened a small door near his seat and pulled out a baby alligator—only nine inches long! It made a soft *cheep, cheep, cheep* noise that sounded like a bird.

"Awesome!" Matthew cheered as Captain René gently brought the alligator out of the box and held it in his hands.

"This *bébé* hatched about two weeks ago," Captain René informed the group. "Her teeth are tiny now. And those yellow stripes on her back will fade as she gets bigger. Who wants to hold her?"

"Me! Me! Me!" said Matthew excitedly. Captain René smiled and showed him how to hold the alligator. Dad began snapping pictures.

"This is the coolest thing ever!" exclaimed Matthew.

"Hey, how about you two?" Dad said, looking at the twins. "You'll hold the alligator, right?"

"No *way!*" Amanda said forcefully as Molly said, "Absolutely!" at the same time. Everyone laughed, especially Dad.

"Sounds like 'the twin thing' is a little out of sync!" Dad joked. Captain René took the alligator from Matthew and transferred it to Molly.

"Come on, Manda," Molly coaxed. "You might never get the chance to hold a baby alligator again. And if *Matthew* can do it, you can!"

"Oh, *fine,*" Amanda said, squeezing her eyes closed as Molly gingerly handed her the alligator. "Whoa—it feels so smooth!" Dad snapped another picture, and Amanda looked at Captain René. "Um, do you want it back now?"

"It's a good thing Dad got that picture," Molly joked. "Otherwise *nobody* would believe that Manda actually held an alligator!"

chapter 8

After the Moores returned to Rivet Mansion, everyone took a quick shower and got ready for dinner. Mom and Dad had made a reservation for the whole family at one of their favorite New Orleans restaurants, Château Savoie.

When they were all ready, the Moores went outside and Dad hailed a cab. "Château Savoie, please," he told the driver. "It's in the French Quarter."

On the trip to the restaurant, Mom told the twins, "The French Quarter is one of the oldest parts of New Orleans. Many of the buildings there are landmarks, and many of them are at least one hundred fifty years old!"

The restaurant was beautiful. It had pale gold walls that were illuminated by old-fashioned gas lamps, which gave off a soft, gentle glow. The wooden floor creaked a little as the maître d' led the Moores to their table next to a big window.

"Well, the menu's changed a bit, but the restaurant looks the same," Mom said after glancing at her menu. "The food is *wonderful*, kids. We should definitely order the shrimp remoulade.

"Mom, what's remoulade?" Molly asked.

"Oh, it's a delicious sauce made with mustard, mayonnaise, capers, celery, garlic, horseradish—lots of good flavors."

Matthew scrunched up his nose. "Ewww. I want a hamburger."

Just then, the waiter came over. He had overheard Matthew's remark and he smiled broadly. "Well, it's not what Château Savoie is known for, but I think we can make up a hamburger for this young man," he said jovially. "My name is Shane, and I'll be your waiter for this evening. May I suggest the chicken and andouille sausage gumbo?"

Mom nodded encouragingly at the twins, so they both decided to order that. Dad ordered the chicken Creole, which was served with a spicy red sauce over rice, and Mom had catfish courtbouillon, which was a dish made of catfish, vegetables, and spiced tomato sauce over rice. Matthew, of course, ordered a plain hamburger and french fries. The hamburger looked funny when it arrived on a fancy china plate with a garnish! Mom was right about the food, though—the shrimp remoulade appetizer was delicious, and the twins had never tasted anything like the spicy gumbo before.

During the meal, Molly noticed how Mom and Dad kept smiling at each other. She couldn't help feeling that they were sharing some amusing secret. "What's up with you guys?" she finally asked.

"Nothing," Dad said quickly—a little *too* quickly. He and Mom smiled at each other again.

"Well, to be honest, we have another surprise planned for tonight. But you'll have to wait to find out what it is," Mom added.

Molly and Amanda kept looking around the restaurant, waiting for the "surprise" to show up. As Shane cleared away the last of their meal, they began to suspect that maybe the surprise was that there was no surprise! Until, that is, a tall man in chef's whites appeared at the table. "Girls, meet your surprise," Mom said.

They looked up at the dark-haired, broad-shouldered man, and knew they'd seen him before. But where? Molly was the first to realize who he was. She gasped. "It's Chef Alain—from the Cooking Channel!"

He smiled a wide smile. "You got me! Hi, girls!"

Amanda bounced excitedly in her seat. "Chef Alain! I can't believe it! I love your show! You are so hysterically funny! *Ohmigosh!*" Everyone laughed.

"It's a pleasure to meet you, too," replied Chef Alain. He clapped his hands together. "Now, I've been told that you two girls are successful chefs in your own right, and that you even have your own cooking business. Is this true?"

"Yes," replied Molly, beaming. Amanda could only blush.

"Good! I'm always interested in meeting chefs and hearing their opinions on our food. Would you young ladies be interested in touring the kitchen and sharing your professional opinion of tonight's meal?"

"Oh, could we?" Amanda cried.

"Of course," replied Mom, smiling. "We planned this when we made our reservation!"

The girls leapt up from their seats, and Chef Alain whisked them off through swinging double doors at the back of the dining room. They entered a world of stainless-steel counters, huge stoves, and ceiling-high refrigerators, where cooks and their assistants rapidly prepared the gourmet meals. While the dining area of the restaurant looked old-fashioned, everything in the kitchen was state-of-the-art.

"Wow!" Molly said, wide-eyed.

"Who are these darling young ladies?" asked a dark-haired woman in chef's whites.

"*Salut*, Marie," Chef Alain greeted her. "Girls, this is my sister, Marie. We're the co-owners and executive chefs here. Marie, meet Amanda and Molly Moore. They're up-and-coming chefs, and I'm giving them a tour."

"How wonderful!" Marie cried. "You're like my brother and me, siblings who love to cook!"

Molly pictured Amanda and herself all grown-up and dressed in chef's whites, running their very own restaurant. "That would be so cool to have our own restaurant!"

"Well, an important first step is figuring out what kind of food you want to serve," Chef Alain explained. "Château Savoie has been in our family for many years. We've always specialized in the freshest, most authentic Creole cuisine in New Orleans, if I do say so myself."

"What's Creole?" Amanda asked.

"You're looking at one!" Marie said proudly. "People argue about who's a Creole and who isn't. The simplest explanation I can give is to say that Creoles are people descended from the original Spanish or French settlers, and perhaps also from the African and Caribbean people who lived here."

Amanda spotted vegetables sizzling in a pan. "Were these vegetables blanched before you sautéed them?"

"Yes, but only for a few moments," Marie replied. Looking impressed, she said to Alain, "This young lady knew that I put these vegetables in boiling water before cooking them."

"You do it to brighten the color and make them just a little more tender, right?" Molly added.

"Very good," Alain said.

"Are you enjoying your trip so far?" Marie asked. "Where are you staying?"

"We're staying at Rivet Mansion. New Orleans is *amazing!*" raved Amanda. Molly opened her mouth to agree, but she was interrupted.

"Well, now, what's all this?" The twins spun around to

see a small table set for one in a corner of the kitchen.
Sitting there was a man in an expensive-looking dark suit
with a crimson silk handkerchief peeking out of the
breast pocket. In front of him was a generous serving of
chicken and andouille sausage gumbo, the same
dish the twins had eaten for dinner. "Honestly,
the busboys get younger every year!" the man
said. Molly and Amanda couldn't tell if he was joking or
not. He was smiling, but his dark eyes seemed cold.

"Mind your manners, Claude," Alain scolded him
teasingly, still smiling his famous grin. "These are two of
our guests, Molly and Amanda Moore. They're visiting
chefs, and a credit to the culinary arts!" He turned to the
girls. "Forgive my friend, Claude Doucet. He's one of our
oldest, dearest friends, and a true *gourmand*, one who
loves gourmet food. As a matter of fact, Claude owns this
building, and he eats here nearly every night! That's why
he has a private table here in the back."

"Oh, these girls know I was only joking," Claude said in a smooth, even voice.
"It is a great pleasure to meet you, Chef
Molly and Chef Amanda. Have you had
dessert yet?" The girls shook their heads. He beckoned for
them to follow him out of the kitchen. "Alain, Marie, allow
me to treat them to something from the dessert cart—the
most wonderful desserts in all of New Orleans! Marie is
the head pastry chef here, and she is beyond compare."

"*Merci,*" Marie said sweetly. "Thank you, Claude!"

"Oh, wait!" Molly said, blushing slightly. "Um, Chef Alain, could we have your autograph?"

"*Molly!*" exclaimed Amanda. *That's so uncool,* she thought.

But Chef Alain just smiled. "My pleasure, Chef Molly," he said. Molly checked her pockets for paper but found none. Then she noticed a slip of paper on the floor. She picked it up and, still blushing, handed it to Chef Alain.

With a flourish, he wrote "Best of luck to two fine chefs, Molly and Amanda—Alain Savoie." Molly tucked the autograph safely in the MetroCard holder she always carried around in her pocket.

Chef Alain and Claude walked the twins to their family's table in the dining room, followed by Shane, who was pushing a large cart piled high with a gorgeous array of desserts. "The entire family will be our guests for dessert," Chef Alain announced, "since Mr. and Mrs. Moore are celebrating their anniversary."

"*Oooh,* can we each get one and share? So everyone can try a different kind?" cried Amanda. "I don't know what I want—it all looks so good! Wait, I know, I want the chocolate crepes with berries!" Her family giggled at her enthusiasm. Nobody loved sweets as much as Amanda!

"This was, like, the *perfect* day in New Orleans!" Molly said excitedly. "Thanks, Mom and Dad."

"Yeah, thanks so much," echoed Amanda. Matthew

couldn't say anything—his mouth was already stuffed
with rich chocolate doberge cake.

The next morning at breakfast, there was a cream-
colored envelope next to Amanda's plate that read "Miss
Amanda Moore" in calligraphy. There was
another envelope waiting at Molly's
plate that read "Miss Molly Moore."

"What's this—another surprise?"
Molly asked Mom and Dad. But they seemed as clueless
as Molly and Amanda. The twins looked at each other
and shrugged, then ripped open the envelopes.

Dear Miss Moore,
        Alain and I were delighted to meet you and your
sister last night. We were very impressed by your pas-
sion for cooking and would like to invite you to assist us
today as we prepare a banquet dinner for the educational
conference being held in New Orleans. If you are able
to attend, please join us at the restaurant at 10:00 a.m.
As the front doors will be locked, please use the service
entrance in the back.

                                        Cordially yours,
                                        Marie Savoie

"Can we? Please?" Molly asked after she read the letter aloud.

"I don't see why not," Dad agreed.

"What a fabulous opportunity!" Mom said proudly.

Dad turned to Matthew so he wouldn't feel left out. "What would you like to do today, buddy? It's just you and me. How about the Children's Museum?" Matthew nodded happily in agreement.

Molly and Amanda grinned at each other. This trip was getting better and better!

"Come in, come in," Marie greeted Molly and Amanda as they walked into the kitchen of Château Savoie. "Before we do anything, I must give you these." She came out from behind a long table and handed each of the girls a stack of folded white cloth. "Your own chef's whites."

"Awesome!" Amanda cried. "Thanks so much!"

"Yes, thank you," Molly added.

The twins went to a bathroom to change and emerged looking and feeling like real chefs. Alain came into the kitchen and clapped his hands together when he saw them. "Perfect!" he exclaimed.

For the first hour, each twin received a cooking lesson.

Marie showed Amanda how to make a *gâteau de sirop,* a rich, classic Cajun cake made with spices and dark Louisiana cane syrup. Alain revealed the secret of his special meat rubs to Molly.

"Now, if you don't mind, we'll put you to work doing some of the chores that every apprentice—the *commis*—must do," Alain said. "The *commis* is an entry-level position in the restaurant business that involves peeling, chopping, and prep work."

"No problem," Molly assured him.

The basic cooking skills the twins had learned in their summer class at Park Terrace Cookware came in handy. Alain complimented Molly and Amanda on their knife skills before moving to another station in the kitchen, where he concentrated on the main course for the banquet, chicken Creole. Amanda kept glancing over at Marie at the pastry station, where she seemed to be effortlessly creating the most lavish, gorgeous desserts. The kitchen was full of people, all of them focused and intent. The twins had never realized that it took so much effort to run a restaurant.

The afternoon flew by, and suddenly it was five o'clock. Dad had arrived to pick up the twins.

"Look at you two," said Dad, chuckling. "You're covered in food!" He smiled at the girls. "Finish up—I'll be right out front."

Marie and Alain came over to the girls. "Thank

you so much for your help," Alain said warmly. The twins beamed.

"We had a great time!" exclaimed Molly. "We'll be back at eight o'clock for the banquet. I can't wait!"

"Yes, thanks so much for letting us help," Amanda added.

At that moment, Claude Doucet walked into the kitchen. He stopped abruptly when he saw the twins, and an ugly scowl darkened his face.

Yipes, Molly thought. *What's his problem?*

"Alain, a word," Claude said sharply. Chef Alain said good-bye to the twins and walked over to Claude. As the twins left the kitchen, they heard Claude hiss, "What are you doing? *Children* in the *kitchen?* Do you need to be reminded that this is a professional restaurant? Their presence is entirely inappropriate!"

Both twins, embarrassed, started to blush.

"Relax, Claude," Chef Alain said softly, glancing at the twins as they hurried out. They heard him say, "They've had a lot of experience and they were closely supervised," just as the kitchen door closed behind them.

"What was that about?" Amanda asked, confused.

"I don't care how much dessert that Claude tries to buy us," Molly said as they walked out onto the busy street to join Dad. "I don't like him."

chapter 9

"**Y**ou girls look lovely," Mom said as she met up with the family at Château Savoie later that night for the conference dinner. Molly was wearing black satin capri pants and a matching spaghetti-strap top that she had borrowed from Amanda. Amanda wore a long black skirt with a side slit and a sparkly red top with short sleeves.

Every few steps Mom waved to one of the professors she knew from the conference. "The conference is going well," she said. "And I'm so glad that you're all with me!"

"We're glad, too," Molly answered. "Today was the best. I hope everyone likes the food!"

"It'll be delicious," Amanda replied confidently. "Alain and Marie are awesome. Listen, don't you think Alain's TV show would be better if he had two adorable guest chefs who helped him cook? Think of it, 'And now, the Kids' Cooking Corner with Amanda and Molly Moore!' Isn't that a good idea?"

"Not bad," Molly said, laughing. "But maybe it should be called the Kids' Cooking Corner with *Molly* and Amanda Moore!"

The Moores found their table and sat down. The twins had to listen to several boring speeches, but finally it was time for dinner to be served. Waiters in tuxedos and waitresses in black dresses emerged from the kitchen carefully balancing large trays of creamy crawfish gumbo, salads, and appetizers. Marie and Alain entered the room, no longer in their chef's whites. Marie wore a long, elegant dress and Alain was wearing a distinguished dark suit. People applauded as they walked to the microphone that had been set up for the speeches.

Alain spoke into the microphone. "Thank you very much. My sister Marie and I hope that you will enjoy your meal. But before you begin, we would like to thank Molly and Amanda Moore for their invaluable help in preparing it." Alain and Marie started to clap.

Molly and Amanda couldn't believe it! They blushed as the people in the restaurant applauded.

"Stand up, girls," Mom encouraged them.

"That was so cool!" Amanda said as she and Molly sat back down. "The crowd loves us. We'd be great on Alain's show!"

"Well, I can't wait to taste this food. The gumbo looks wonderful," Dad said. He lifted his spoon to his mouth while the twins watched with proud smiles, waiting for his reaction.

But instead of telling the girls how good the soup tasted, a horrified expression crossed Dad's face and he quickly reached for his glass of water.

"Ugh!" someone yelled. "This is *awful!"*

A woman jumped up from her table. "This soup—I think it's been poisoned!" she cried.

"Poisoned?" a man exclaimed.

"It's not poison," Molly insisted. She raised her spoon to taste it, to show everyone that the food she'd helped prepare was *delicious.*

Mom grabbed her arm to stop her. "Don't eat anything until we find out what's going on."

But Amanda had already taken a bite. An expression of disgust twisted her face—the taste was so awful, so bitter, that she was unable to even speak. She spit the mouthful of soup back into her bowl and reached for her glass of soda.

"Sorry," Amanda said, embarrassed. "I know that was totally gross and rude. But I *could not* swallow that soup! Yuck!"

Mom went to her, worried. "Do you feel all right?"

Amanda stuck her tongue out. "I feel okay. It just tasted disgusting."

How could this have happened? Molly wondered. *Manda and I were in the kitchen almost all day. All the ingredients were fresh!*

Still standing at the microphone, Marie and Alain were wide-eyed with shock. Then Alain charged back into the kitchen, followed closely by Marie.

"I have to find out what happened!" Molly said, leaving the table.

"Molly! Come back!" Mom called, but Molly didn't hear her.

In the kitchen, Alain had just sampled the soup. "This is a disaster!" he shouted. "How could this have happened? I tasted the soup an hour ago and it was fine!"

Marie was standing near him, talking rapidly on a cordless phone. "Yes, I'm calling from Château Savoie in the French Quarter. Someone has tampered with our food—ruined it! Please send the police right away." Her face clouded over as she said the next sentence in a low voice. "And you'd better send an ambulance, too—we don't know what was put in the food."

Just then, Claude came into the kitchen. "You need to go back to the dining room right away," he told Molly. "A restaurant kitchen is no place for children."

Molly felt her face flush with anger and embarrassment. Reeling around, she slammed her palms against the swinging doors and hurried out of the kitchen. At the table she told her family about what was going on in the kitchen. As she finished her story, she could hear sirens in the distance.

"Mom, this is so bad," Amanda said tearfully. She was starting to feel really freaked out. "What if there's something in the food? What if I'm gonna get sick?"

"Don't worry, sweetie," Mom said reassuringly. "You didn't swallow any of it. We'll get to the bottom of this."

"I'm so hungry!" complained Matthew.

"Can we go back to the hotel?" Amanda asked.

"I don't think we can do that just yet," Dad said seriously as several police officers entered the room. Molly and Amanda looked at each other worriedly. They had never expected anything like *this* to happen.

For the next two hours, no one was allowed to leave the restaurant. A medical team gave people a quick checkup and pronounced everyone fine, while the police recorded the name and hotel address of every person in the room. Somebody ordered crawfish pizzas and jambalaya from another restaurant to feed all the hungry people who were forced to stay at Château Savoie. The kitchen was sealed off with bright yellow crime-scene tape. Inside, several detectives and lab analysts searched for clues and took samples of all the food. Then the twins overheard someone say that the restaurant kitchen was being dusted for fingerprints.

Molly turned to Amanda with wide eyes. "Manda! Our fingerprints will be all over the place!"

"*Ohmigosh,*" breathed Amanda.

A scary thought hit the twins at the same time. *Will we be suspects?*

chapter 10

The next morning, Molly and Amanda woke up exhausted and were still upset about what had happened the day before. They hadn't returned to Rivet Mansion until almost midnight, but even then they were too keyed up to sleep.

When they went downstairs for breakfast, Molly spotted a copy of the Sunday *New Orleans Herald* on the dining room table. Immediately, the headline caught her eye.

POPULAR RESTAURANT INVESTIGATED

Château Savoie, the popular Creole restaurant in the French Quarter owned by celebrity chef Alain Savoie and his sister, Marie Savoie, is closed today pending the investigation of an apparent food tampering that occurred last night. A banquet held for visiting professors attending the Future of Education conference was ruined when an unidentified substance was added to the meal. Though final analysis of the substance is still pending, preliminary toxicology reports found that it was nontoxic. Nonetheless, the extreme bitterness of the dishes rendered the meal inedible. "No one could eat it," said a visibly distressed Chef Alain, host of the popular cable cooking show, *Southern Chef.* An anonymous police source stated that the building's owner, Claude Doucet, informed authorities that two out-of-town guest chefs helped prepare the meal.

"*Ohmigosh!*" Molly cried out. "We're suspects! They think we messed up the food!"

Amanda grabbed the paper from her and started reading.

Meanwhile, Mom and Dad had opened another newspaper to the story. "This is ridiculous," Mom said angrily. "Who would ever think two girls would be involved in this?"

"That Claude Doucet has some nerve," Dad said.

"Don't worry, girls," Mom said firmly. "Nothing will come of this."

Madame Rivet's gaze fixed on something in the doorway. Two men were standing there, surveying the group. "I hope you are right," Madame Rivet said in a low voice to Mrs. Moore, "because there are two detectives in my dining room."

"Wow! Cops!" Matthew said, impressed. "Mom, are Amanda and Molly going to jail?"

"Matthew!" Mom scolded. "They haven't done

anything wrong and they are *not* going to jail."

Amanda bit her lip, worried. The woman seated to her left patted her arm kindly. "Don't worry, dear—your mother's right. This will all work out." But Amanda was still concerned.

Madame Rivet rose from her chair. "Let me go see what they want."

Everyone at the table watched her approach the detectives. Molly swallowed hard when Madame Rivet nodded over toward the Moores, then waved for the five of them to join her. "These men would like to interview you about the problem at the restaurant last night," she said. "Let me show you all to the parlor." She led the two men and the twins, Matthew, and their parents to a sunny sitting room to the right of the front desk.

"I'm Detective Blanchard. This is my partner, Detective Landry. As you girls know, your fingerprints are all over the restaurant's kitchen," said the first detective, a short, balding man. "But let me assure you that we have no reason to consider you suspects."

Sure you don't, Molly thought skeptically.

"I should hope not!" Mom said. "They're just children!"

"We want to talk to you because you were in the kitchen during the day," said Detective Landry, a tall white-haired man. "Claude Doucet told us you two were cooking. Did you see anything unusual?"

"We didn't really cook," Molly said. "Mostly we helped peel and chop vegetables. I don't know why Mr. Doucet said we were cooking."

"Did anyone else come in?" the tall detective asked. The girls shook their heads. "Did you see anything unusual at all?"

The twins shrugged and replied that they hadn't. Detective Blanchard handed Mr. Moore a business card. "Call us if you remember anything," he said to the twins. The detectives then thanked them and left.

"This is outrageous," Mom said. "How could they question two girls? What a waste of time!"

"They're just doing their job, I guess," Dad said.

"I want to go to Château Savoie right now and ask Claude why he thought we were involved," Molly said. "That makes me really mad!"

"No, girls," Mom said firmly. "Stay away from that restaurant. I think we should just enjoy the rest of our vacation."

"I agree," Dad said. "And if those detectives come around again, don't talk to them unless you're with Mom or me. Now, let's finish breakfast and get on with our day."

After breakfast, Mom had to attend several meetings, so Dad and the kids took the Riverfront streetcar along the Mississippi River to the Audubon Aquarium of the Americas. The aquarium had hundreds of different species of fish and even an area that re-created the Amazon rain forest, with a twenty-foot waterfall. Matthew ran from tank to tank, wide-eyed with excitement. Every other word out of his mouth was "Wow!" or "Look!" But even though they tried to enjoy the aquarium, Molly and Amanda couldn't really get into it.

"What are you thinking about?" Amanda asked Molly as the girls gazed into a shark tank.

"Château Savoie," Molly said glumly.

"Me, too," Amanda admitted with a sigh. "Mom said to forget it, but I just can't. What do you think we should do?"

"I don't know," Molly said. "But we've got to do *something*."

"Hey, Mom?" asked Molly that night after dinner, with Amanda standing quietly behind her.

"Yes?"

"Can we use your laptop? We need to e-mail Peichi. And we wanna tell all of the Chef Girls about what happened at Château Savoie."

Mom shook her head. "Sorry, girls, but I have a big presentation tomorrow, and need to use the computer. You can use it tomorrow afternoon, once the presentation's over."

"Oh, okay," Amanda said with a sigh. She turned to

Molly. "Want to hang out downstairs?" Molly shrugged and nodded.

The twins trudged down to the parlor. Amanda plopped into an antique burgundy velvet chair, while Molly sat on an ottoman near her. They saw Isabelle walk near the doorway. The twins smiled as she stopped and waved.

"Hi, girls," said Isabelle. "How is everything? Have the police been back?" Her gray-blue eyes twinkled as she teased the twins.

Molly smiled back. "Okay, I guess. It's just weird, you know."

"It *is* weird," Isabelle agreed. "I was hoping I'd run into you. I'd love to hear more about what happened Saturday night."

The twins recounted their experiences at the restaurant. Isabelle shook her head when she heard how Claude had implied that Molly and Amanda had sabotaged the meal. After they finished their story, Molly mentioned how annoying it was to not have access to a computer.

"We're, like, *dying* to e-mail our friends about all of this!" exclaimed Amanda.

"Why don't you come upstairs and use the computer in my room?" Isabelle offered.

"Wow! Thanks," said Molly, and the twins followed Isabelle to her room. To get there, they had to pass through the kitchen and walk down a long, empty hallway. The twins realized that this part of the mansion—the family's living space—was separate from the hotel.

"*That* explains it!" Molly announced triumphantly.

"What?" asked Isabelle as she and Amanda turned to look at Molly. Molly blushed as she realized that she had spoken out loud.

"Um...Manda and I were, well, wondering why no guests could go into the east wing. And I just realized why—because that's where you guys *live*. Right?"

"Right," Isabelle agreed with a warm smile. "But I figured you two knew that already—especially since I found your barrette in the passageway!"

Now it was Amanda's turn to blush. "Sorry about that," she said. "We were just...curious."

"Hey, it's cool." Isabelle winked at the twins. "I would have done the same thing!" She opened a door at the far end of the hallway.

"The computer is over there on the desk," Isabelle said, pointing. The twins looked around the pretty room. It was painted robin's-egg blue with crisp white trim. Three large windows revealed a view of New Orleans. While the rest of the hotel was old-fashioned and full of antiques, Isabelle's room was completely modern, with sleek furniture and a state-of-the-art CD player and computer. The twins sat at the computer and clicked onto the Internet. They had received two e-mails—one from Natasha and one from Peichi.

To: mooretimes2
From: BrooklynNatasha
Re: Uh-oh...

———————————————

Hey Molly and Amanda!

What's up? How's your trip? I hope U R bringing back lots of recipes for us 2 try!

Dad took me 2 the hardware store today and guess what! We bought purple paint! Tomorrow he's gonna help me paint my room and Shawn and Peichi are coming over to paint, too. I wish you guys could be at the painting party 2. ☹ Oh, well.

Listen, the cheerleader sleepover was a DISASTER. I feel so sorry for Elizabeth. It was totally rotten. I'll tell you EVERYTHING when you get home.

Miss you lots! Have fun!

Natasha

P.S. Wait til you hear what happened 2 Peichi—SO funny!

"Why won't she tell us now?" asked Molly, absent-mindedly clicking "Save as New." Amanda shrugged. Molly clicked on the next e-mail, which was from Peichi.

Molly! Amanda! Ohmigosh!!!

You will NEVER believe what happened . . . this is so weird, I don't even know what 2 do, PLEASE COME HOME SOON so you can give me some advice!!!

Argh. Okay. So, Omar invited me 2 this movie thing, and I thought it was a group of kids who were going. But when I got 2 the movie theater, just Omar was there. And I was all, "Oh, I guess no one else is here yet." And Omar says, "Um, well, no one else is coming." CAN YOU BELIEVE IT? Omar invited JUST me! AAAHHHHHH!

So I tried 2 stay cool even though I was really flipping out, and I said, "Oh, okay." But I was thinking, Does Omar think this is a DATE or something? So then we went inside and we bought our tickets and got some food. I kept thinking, I hope we don't run into anybody from school, and Omar acted totally weird, trying 2 catch popcorn

103

in his mouth, like that's funny or something. I don't remember anything about the movie cuz I just kept thinking, What if Omar tries 2 hold my hand or tells the whole school we went on a DATE? I was still freaking!

So after the movie Omar walked me home, and we didn't really say anything the whole way. It was totally awkward. And we got 2 my house and I was like, Eeek, I hope he doesn't try 2 KISS me. He didn't—but he did SHAKE MY HAND, hahahaha!

So that's the whole long, embarrassing story. I'm totally dreading going back 2 school next week. What will I do if he tells everyone we went on a date?

Hope you 2 are having more fun than I am. ☹

Love, Peichi

"We better get back to New York quick," Amanda said with a laugh. "Things are falling apart without us!"

"I think so, too," Molly agreed.

Isabelle stood up. "I'm going to get some snacks. I'll be right back."

 The twins were almost finished writing an e-mail to their friends when Isabelle returned with a large bowl of hot buttered popcorn and three sodas.

"Have you guys heard zydeco music before?" Isabelle asked as she searched for a CD. The twins shook their heads. "It's awesome Cajun music. Here, listen." Isabelle found the CD she had been looking for and popped it into the player. Loud, upbeat sounds of an accordion filled the room. Zydeco was like jazz and folk and blues all rolled into one. Molly and Amanda smiled at each other—they had never heard anything quite like it. Without thinking, Molly started tapping her foot in time to the music.

"You like it!" Isabelle exclaimed. She pulled Molly and Amanda up from the bed and said, "Come on, I'll show you some dance steps. We'll do the Mamou jitterbug!"

"The *Mamou jitterbug?*" the twins repeated together. Laughing, Molly and Amanda followed Isabelle and found themselves swinging and spinning around the room to the happy zydeco songs. They had forgotten all about the troubles at Château Savoie...for now, at least.

c h a p t e r 11

On Monday morning, the twins grabbed the paper away from Dad's place as soon as they got to the dining room. "I wonder if there's any new info about Château Savoie," Molly said, skimming the front page.

"Look—another article!" said Amanda, spotting the headline before Molly did. "Check this out—'Cursed Château'." The twins silently read the article.

"It says here that there were bitters in the food," said Molly.

"Yeah, it really *was* bitter," Amanda replied, still reading.

"No!" said Molly. "Read this!"

Amanda looked to where Molly was pointing and read out loud. "'Officials have identified the substance in the food as bitters. Bitters are a natural substance, derived from herbs, with a harsh, acrid taste. They are commonly used in minute amounts in cooking, and to keep pets from chewing on furniture or cords.'"

"Then the article says that there was an electrical fire at Chateau Savoie last month," Molly interrupted her. "The restaurant had to close and give free dinners to everyone who was in the dining room. *And* there have been problems with produce deliveries that have interfered with the daily specials."

"It doesn't sound like an accident to me," Amanda said suspiciously.

"It sounds like sabotage," said Isabelle, who had been listening from her seat beside Madame Rivet. After everyone had read the article and eaten breakfast, Mrs. Moore announced that she had to leave for the conference. Dad and Matthew wanted to go to a minor-league baseball game.

"Do you girls want to go to the baseball game?" asked Mr. Moore. Molly thought the ballgame sounded like a pretty good idea, but Amanda wrinkled her nose and shook her head.

"I could show you some cool little boutiques in the French Quarter," Isabelle offered. "I need to pick up a present for my roommate."

"That would be great!" Amanda cried happily.

Suddenly Molly changed her mind about the baseball game. Château Savoie was in the French Quarter. If they went shopping there, they'd probably pass the restaurant...and maybe find out more about the mystery!

"I want to go, too," Molly blurted.

"*You* want to go shopping?" Mrs. Moore asked suspiciously.

"Yeah, what's so bizarre about that?" Molly asked.

Mrs. Moore looked at her daughter as if she didn't

quite believe her. "Well...I want you two to stay with Isabelle at all times, okay? No wandering off."

"Okay!" chorused Molly and Amanda.

The twins and Isabelle left the table and set off for the French Quarter. After stopping in several shops, where the twins bought little gifts for Shawn, Peichi, and Natasha, they came to Château Savoie.

"Wow! Look at that sign," Isabelle pointed to a large notice on the restaurant door: "CLOSED UNTIL FURTHER NOTICE."

"That's awful," Amanda said softly.

"Let's go back to the kitchen and see if Alain and Marie are around," Molly suggested. Amanda started to object, but Molly and Isabelle had already taken off, so reluctantly she followed them. The girls could hear voices coming from the kitchen that sounded like they belonged to Alain and Claude.

"Get out of Château Savoie, Alain. It's going to ruin your good name," Claude was saying. "Close up shop and open a new restaurant. In another city!"

"But I can't, Claude. This restaurant has been in my family for over fifty years! I can't just let it go like that," Alain replied desperately. "And if I give up the restaurant, I could lose my television show. I would be ruined as a chef—ruined."

"No, Alain, no. It'll be all right. I'll help however I can. I can use my connections to help you open a new place, in another city. And I'll let you out of the remaining eight years on the lease. Think, Alain. You must protect yourself, even if it means sacrificing Château Savoie."

"Well, I still don't know..." said Alain doubtfully. "If we catch the culprit I can keep the restaurant and everything will go back to normal."

The girls jumped at a loud noise that sounded like someone banging his fist on the table. "Alain! You're not listening! This is a losing venture in *every way*. Stop denying the obvious." Claude's voice was raised. He didn't sound supportive anymore.

"We'd better go," whispered Amanda. "We don't want to get caught out here. Claude suspects us enough already." The three crept silently to the front of the building. As they reached the sidewalk, Marie came out the front door. The twins and Isabelle jumped.

"Oh, hi," Marie said. "I hope I didn't startle you."

"We've been shopping," Amanda said quickly. "Here in the French Quarter."

Isabelle stepped forward and offered her hand to Marie. "My name is Isabelle Rivet. I'm so sorry about Château Savoie's misfortunes."

Marie smiled sadly and started taking down the crime-scene tape. After a moment, she spoke. "The Château may be closing for good. After everything that's gone wrong, I don't think that we can take any more bad publicity. Have you been reading the papers?"

CRIME SCENE: DO NOT CROSS

"Yeah...and there's something I don't get. If bitters are normally used in cooking, why did the food taste so terrible?" Molly asked. "And why do people use bitters at all?"

"Well, bitters can add a delightful undertone to sauces and drinks when used properly. But the normal amount is just a single drop. Whoever tampered with the food must have used much, much more than that. And the police found spray bottles containing bitters, so it was very easy for someone to add them to the food at the last minute." Marie stopped and put her hand to her mouth. "I probably shouldn't have said that. Don't repeat it, okay?" The twins nodded. Just then, the front door burst open and Claude strode out angrily.

Yipes! Molly thought. *So much for avoiding Claude.* He didn't even look at the twins, although he must have seen them talking to Marie. He left in a hurry.

The twins and Isabelle said good-bye to Marie and walked down the street—in the opposite direction.

As Amanda and Isabelle chatted about the shops they'd visited, Molly was lost in thought about the mystery at Château Savoie. *I don't trust that Claude guy. He's really mean. But why would he sabotage his best friend's restaurant?* She sighed. *It doesn't make any sense.*

"Check out this one!" cried Amanda, trying on a massive bird costume with trails of teal, purple, and gold feathers flowing out behind her. She attached a wooden beak to her head. Molly carefully put on a jaguar costume. It was gold velvet with black spots, and had a wire tail covered in matching spotted velvet. Molly chased her sister, roaring, while Amanda squawked insanely and ran to hide behind a costume rack. Isabelle laughed so hard she had to sit down.

"Isn't costume shopping for Mardi Gras the best?" said Isabelle.

"Yeah, it's great!" Molly agreed.

"I totally want to come back to New Orleans for Mardi Gras! I can't believe we missed it this year," Amanda said, carefully taking off the bird costume.

"I'm starving. Let's go to Café Du Monde," Isabelle said once they were back in their regular clothes. "There's something I want you to try!"

"Sure!" cried the twins. The three girls walked a few blocks to Café Du Monde. It was very crowded, and it smelled of sugar and coffee. Isabelle ordered beignets for all three of them and a café au lait—coffee mixed with chicory and hot milk—for herself.

"These are *sooo* good!" Amanda exclaimed after taking a bite of the puffy pastry covered with powdered sugar.

"Definitely," agreed Molly. "But they're not that

different from the zeppoles we have in Brooklyn."

"They're totally different!" cried Amanda.

"They're both fried dough with powdered sugar on top," Molly insisted.

"Well, one difference is that beignets are French, and zeppoles are Italian!" Isabelle suggested as she sipped her café au lait.

When they had finished their beignets, Isabelle and the twins walked back to Rivet Mansion. The twins' parents and Matthew were not back yet. Isabelle went to her room to work on a paper. When the twins went to their room, they were surprised to find an envelope shoved under their door.

"It must be another note from Alain or Marie," Amanda said. She opened the envelope. Suddenly she gasped and dropped the paper to the floor. Molly slowly picked up the note and read it. It said:

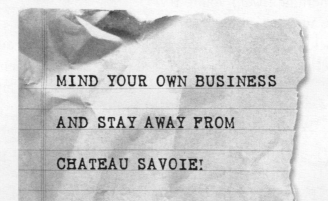

MIND YOUR OWN BUSINESS

AND STAY AWAY FROM

CHATEAU SAVOIE!

chapter 12

"We have to show this to Mom and Dad!" cried Amanda.

"No way. Mom and Dad won't let us do *anything* in New Orleans if they see this."

"But Molls, someone is, like, *watching* us! They know we were at Château Savoie today!" Amanda exclaimed. "This is so creepy!"

"Look, let's just wait a little while," urged Molly. "Otherwise Mom might send us home early with Dad or something."

Before the twins could finish their conversation, Mom returned from the conference.

"Hi, girls," Mom said, standing in the doorway. "How was your day?"

"Great!" exclaimed Molly, slipping the note in her pocket.

"We tried on Mardi Gras costumes. It was awesome!" Amanda told her.

"That sounds fun! Listen, Dad and Matthew should be home any minute, so wash up and get ready for dinner. We're going to a wonderful restaurant called Jacques-Imo's. It's very famous."

"We'll change right now!" Molly said as Mom went to her room. Amanda put on a light blue dress, and Molly chose black pants and a green peasant top. They couldn't stop talking about the scary note while they were getting ready.

"Amanda—let's go downstairs before Mom and Dad finish getting dressed and ask Madame Rivet if she saw anyone near our room today," Molly suggested.

"Good idea," Amanda agreed. She called her parents' room to tell them that she and Molly would meet them downstairs. The twins found Madame Rivet in the parlor, arranging some fresh flowers.

"Madame Rivet?" asked Molly. "Um, did anyone...strange...come in the hotel today? Or ask which room Amanda and I are staying in?"

Madame Rivet frowned. "*Pardon?* No, Molly, not that I know of. Why do you ask? Would you like me to speak to the porters about it?"

"No, thanks," Molly said. "It's no big deal. I was just, um, wondering." She saw her parents and Matthew coming downstairs. "I have to go. See you later!" The twins met the rest of the family at the front door, and the Moores left Rivet Mansion for Jacques-Imo's.

Jacques-Imo's was different from all of the other restaurants the Moores had eaten at in New Orleans—it had a fun, casual atmosphere, with red and green lights gleaming outside the front door. The restaurant was so crowded that the Moores had a little trouble squeezing past all of the people in the front section to reach the dining room in the back. The walls were painted with murals of swampland, and the wooden tables in the dining room were crammed tightly together. As soon as the Moores sat at one, a young man brought them a basket of warm, crumbly cornbread with butter.

"Hi, my name's Francis and I'll be your waiter tonight. Our special is black drum Creole, prepared with a sauce of peppers, tomato, and garlic with a touch of Tabasco."

"Yuck! You serve *drums* here? Like the kind you play?" Matthew said in alarm.

Mrs. Moore laughed. "No, Matthew, a drum is a kind of a fish. Would you like to try it, kids?"

Matthew shook his head violently. "I want fried chicken," he said firmly.

"I'll try the drum!" Amanda said, giggling.

"Me, too!" Molly chimed in.

Dad smiled proudly at the girls and then turned to Matthew. "Come on, sport! The whole point of going on vacation is trying new things!" Matthew shook his head and crossed his arms. Mom shrugged and turned to the waiter.

"So I guess that will be one order of fried chicken and four black drum Creoles." Mom smiled slyly at Dad. "And two orders of alligator cheesecake—for everyone to share!" Francis nodded and left.

Amanda and Molly's jaws dropped. "No way are we eating alligator!" Molly cried.

"Yeah! *Alligator* in *cheesecake?* That's a terrible thing to do to cheesecake!" Amanda said, wrinkling her nose.

Before Mr. Moore could reply, Matthew said, "I'll try it. Eating an alligator sounds cool." The rest of the family looked at him in surprise.

"We can't let Matthew make us look like babies," Molly said. "We *have* to try it now."

"Okay," Amanda agreed reluctantly. "We'll try the alligator cheesecake, too."

Francis was soon back with the alligator cheesecake, and the kids were surprised to discover that it was an appetizer, not a dessert. It was like a cream-cheese quiche with alligator and shrimp—and it tasted terrific! Soon after they had finished, Francis arrived with their main courses, and they dug in eagerly.

"This black drum is delicious," Dad said, wiping his mouth. "What do you think, girls? You're pretty quiet over there."

The twins glanced at each other. They had both been lost in thought—about Marie taking down the crime-scene tape, about Claude and Alain's argument, about the frightening note they'd found in their room.

"It's really yummy," Amanda replied. "We're just tired from today. Too much, um, shopping."

"Yeah," Molly chimed in. "Too much shopping."

On Tuesday, the twins and Matthew stayed at the hotel with Dad to do their make-up homework while Mom attended meetings. Afterward, Dad took the kids to the Carousel Gardens in New Orleans City Park. There they had a picnic lunch, and everyone rode on the antique carousel. Molly and Amanda were both glad to get their minds off Château Savoie.

On Wednesday, Mom had almost the whole day free, so the family decided to explore the city together. They went to a farmers' market that was open twenty-four hours a day and stopped in lots of great antique shops. For lunch, they ate outside at a small café, where Mom and Dad ordered delicious French bread po'boy sandwiches for everyone. Mom and Dad had seafood po'boys made with fried oysters, fried shrimp, shredded lettuce, tomatoes, and pickles. The twins and Matthew had roast beef po'boys with gravy and French fries!

"This French fry sandwich is awesome," Matthew mumbled with his mouth full. "You guys should make this at home for Dish!"

As the family ate, Molly saw a pale young man with black hair staring at them from across the street.

"Manda, look at that guy over there. I think he's watching us!" whispered Molly.

Amanda looked up and saw him. "That's freaky," she murmured.

The girls looked away for a few minutes, and when they turned around again, the black-haired man had disappeared.

By Thursday there were only a few more days left of the trip. It was Mom's last day at the conference, so she was going to be busy all day. At breakfast, the twins were wondering what to do when Madame Rivet spoke up. "Why don't you take your brother on a voodoo tour? You can't possibly leave New Orleans without experiencing one!"

"A voodoo tour?" asked Matthew, his eyes growing wide. "What's voodoo?"

"It's a religion originally from West Africa," replied Madame Rivet. "The real name is actually Voudun, which comes from an African word meaning 'spirit.' Voudun was carried around the world by captured slaves—and that's how it came to New Orleans. It focuses on 'white magic' rituals to bring good fortune and healing. And also from Voudun comes the belief in zombies—dead people who are brought back from beyond the grave."

"And voodoo dolls," Isabelle said. "I haven't been on a voodoo tour in ages. I'll take you guys, if you want to go. And we could check out the old cemeteries, too."

"Awesome!" exclaimed Molly. "We'll totally go!"

"No way!" Matthew stammered. "I mean, I'm not scared, it just sounds, um, boring." But everyone could tell that Matthew really *was* scared.

"Maybe Matthew and I will go to the Audubon Zoo today," Dad said.

Later that morning, Isabelle took the twins to see one of the city's historic cemeteries before the start of the voodoo tour. The sky was overcast, and a cool, wet breeze was blowing. In the cemetery, tall stone monuments stood close together behind iron gates.

"It looks like a city," Amanda said as they walked down pathways between the tombs, some of which were taller than the twins themselves.

"Definitely," agreed Isabelle. "The aboveground tombs have inspired people to call these cemeteries the Cities of the Dead. This one is from the 1800s. The tombs are aboveground because the ground is too wet for burying caskets—they would pop up to the surface whenever it rained. Pretty creepy, isn't it?"

The twins nodded in agreement as they studied the dates and inscriptions on the tombs. Soon it was time for the voodoo tour.

The guide led them around the winding, narrow streets

of the old, historic French Quarter. She was a tall woman of African descent, with long, straight, black hair, and she wore a deep red dress. She pointed out many buildings that had a haunted history of ghosts and bizarre occurrences. And she told the tales in a dramatic, low voice.

The moving clouds overhead threw odd reflections on the wavy, uneven glass of the old windows and cast unexpected shadows on the cobblestone streets. The tour group visited the Voodoo Museum and climbed down narrow stairs to a darkened room where they witnessed a ritual. As musicians pounded drums, a man wearing many shell necklaces danced holding a live snake.

"He'd be a hit at the next Windsor Middle School dance," Molly cracked to Amanda as the guide led them up another set of stairs. Amanda smiled absentmindedly. Ever since the girls had been in the cemetery that morning, she couldn't shake the feeling that the twins were being, well, *watched.*

The rickety stairs led to a room where they saw voodoo dolls and gris-gris bags, which held what were supposed to be magic potions. The guide pointed to a portrait of a stately, attractive African-American woman in a colorful dress with a cloth wrap around her head. "This is Marie Laveau, the famous Voodoo Queen of New Orleans. She was believed to work powerful magic. One of her devoted followers gave her a mansion on Saint Ann Street. Those who didn't believe in spells and charms claimed that her power was due to her network of servants and slaves who spied on the rich and famous for her. This spy network provided her with great influence over local leaders."

After leaving the Voodoo Museum, the tour visited another cemetery with more aboveground tombs. "This cemetery was founded in 1789," the guide told them. "It's on the National Register of Historic Places. It houses the remains of many important figures in New Orleans's past, but most notably, it's the final resting place of Marie Laveau herself."

They walked down the path until they came to a monument that was as tall as the other ones but less formal. It looked like a stone hut. "Marie Laveau is thought to have died in 1881, though many claimed to have seen her after that," the guide said. "It's possible, of course, that they were seeing one of Marie's fifteen children— her daughter, who became a voodoo queen and looked identical to her mother. But there's no way to know for certain, is there?"

Amanda shivered.

Molly noticed that there were many X's chalked on the tomb. "What are these?" she asked the guide.

"Today people still come to ask for Marie Laveau's advice and help," the guide answered. "They say that if you draw three marks, leave a gift, and ask your question, the spirit of Marie Laveau will help you." When the tour ended and the group dispersed, Amanda, Molly, and Isabelle stayed at the foot of Marie Laveau's grave, looking at the chalk X's on the tomb.

Amanda flinched as the leaves on the trees rustled and a cool breeze swept across her face.

"Molls, can we go?" Amanda said in a low voice. "This is weird. I don't like it here."

"Oh, *Amanda*," Molly sighed, rolling her eyes. "It's just a *cemetery*. Don't freak out. None of that scary voodoo stuff is real."

"Boo!" yelled Isabelle, popping out from behind the tomb.

"*Aaagh!*" shrieked Amanda, practically jumping into Molly's arms. Isabelle and Molly collapsed with laughter while Amanda stood there, clutching her heart and breathing heavily.

"You guys!" Amanda cried. "That was *so* not funny!"

"Sorry, Manda!" chuckled Molly. "But you should have seen your face!" All at once, Molly stopped laughing. "Something moved," she whispered. "Over there."

"What?" Amanda asked as she and Isabelle spun around to look where Molly was pointing. Just then, a shadowy figure ducked behind a tomb—but not before the girls recognized that dark hair and ghostly pale skin.

It was the young man who'd been watching them at the café!

"**L**et's get out of here!" Molly whispered sharply.

Amanda took off after her, and Isabelle followed them both, calling, "Wait! What's going on?" They raced down the path, not daring to look back and see whether the man was chasing after them.

But he was. The young man sprinted after them and darted between monuments until somehow, he was standing in front of them on the path, blocking their way.

"Wait! Please!" he said, panting from his run. "I just—I just have to—talk to you."

The girls backed up, keeping their distance from the man. Molly felt certain that he reminded her of someone, but she couldn't figure out who.

"What's going on?" Isabelle asked sharply. She turned to the twins. "Do you know this guy?" she asked

"Please—I'll explain," the man said breathlessly. "I'm sorry I scared you. I'm Chris Savoie."

"As in—Château *Savoie*?" Molly asked. Now she knew who it was he reminded her of—Marie! "Are you related to Marie and Alain?" she asked.

"I'm Marie's son. Chef Alain is my uncle," Chris said. "I need to talk to you about everything that's happened at

123

Château Savoie. Can I buy you something at a café so we can talk? It'll just take a few moments."

Molly and Amanda looked at each other, still cautious. But he certainly did look like a Savoie, and they trusted Marie and Alain.

"All right," Molly agreed. "But Isabelle comes, too."

"You bet I'm coming," Isabelle said firmly.

The four of them left the cemetery and walked to a nearby café. A light rain started to fall, so they quickly hurried inside and found a table near the window.

"Okay, Chris," Isabelle said. "Why don't you explain why you were chasing us."

Chris sighed and looked down at the marble tabletop. "I'm not entirely sure where to begin," he said slowly. "Well, I told you that Marie is my mom, and Alain is my uncle. And I know how worried they've been about the restaurant since all the strange stuff started happening."

"The electrical fire," Molly said, remembering the newspaper article. "And the problems with food deliveries."

"That's right," Chris said. "Mom and Uncle Alain refused to believe it was sabotage—at least, until last Saturday—but I've been suspicious for a while. And when this latest mess happened, I came right home from college. It's the least I can do, you know?"

Molly and Amanda nodded.

"So how can the twins help you?" Isabelle asked.

Chris looked embarrassed. "Well, I'm not completely

sure," he admitted. "All I know is that Claude really dislikes you two. No offense," he added. "I want to know if you did anything—anything at all—to provoke him. Because to be honest, I think Claude is behind all of this. And I think he's trying to use you girls as a distraction."

"We think it's Claude, too," Molly said, sitting forward. "Why do *you* think he's the one?"

"Over winter break I interned at an architecture firm in downtown New Orleans," Chris said. "While I was there, I heard a rumor that Claude received an offer on the building that houses the restaurant. See, he inherited it from his grandfather. My mother and uncle only rent the building from him, but they have a long lease. Claude could make at least a few million by selling the building right now, but he has no way of forcing Uncle Alain and my mother out of their eight-year lease."

"Have you told them all this?" Isabelle asked.

"I mentioned it. But Claude's too smooth. He admitted that he had received an offer, but convinced my mom and my uncle that he turned it down. He put on a big show. They think that Claude is one of their dearest friends, so they believe him. But I've always thought he was a big phony. I have a motive for Claude, but no solid evidence. At this point, my suspicions alone aren't enough to take to the police."

Amanda spoke up "We don't have any evidence against Claude. Believe me, *we* don't like him, either. If we knew *anything* we would have told the police already." Molly nodded sadly.

"That's okay," Chris replied kindly, though he seemed a little disappointed. "But listen, if you *do* think of anything, please let me know." He scribbled on a paper napkin. "Here's my cell phone number. Don't hesitate to contact me." Molly took the napkin, folded it, and tucked it in her MetroCard holder to keep it safe.

No one said much as the twins and Isabelle walked back to Rivet Mansion. The twins thanked Isabelle for taking them on the voodoo tour and went to their room to wait for Mom, Dad, and Matthew. Molly flopped on her bed and took out the napkin with Chris's cell phone number. Another small slip of paper fluttered out of her MetroCard holder and landed on the bed.

"Hey, it's Alain's autograph," Molly said to her sister. "With everything that's happened, I forgot about it!"

"*I* didn't forget," Amanda teased. "You were totally starstruck!"

"Look who's talking," Molly retorted. "Well, we weren't able to help Chef Alain, but we did get his autograph." She turned the paper over in her hand and gasped. "Amanda! Look at this!"

"It's a credit card receipt," Amanda said. "From American Restaurant Supply Incorporated. What's the big deal?"

"It's *Claude's* receipt! It has his signature on it!" Molly shrieked. "For *four bottles of bitters!* Manda! He must have dropped it in the kitchen when he hid the bitters!"

"*Ohmigosh!*" squealed Amanda. "We have to call Chris! We have to call the police!"

Finally, the twins knew without a doubt that Claude was the culprit.

They had proof!

For the next forty-five minutes, Molly and Amanda paced anxiously in the front hallway of the hotel, waiting for their parents and Matthew to get back. They'd told Isabelle right away, and she had called Chris and left a message on his cell phone. Then Isabelle had given the twins an envelope to put the receipt in so that it would be safe. Isabelle sat on the staircase, tapping her foot nervously. Molly sighed deeply. "I can't stand it," she said. "Where *are* they?"

"I'm sure they'll be back soon," Isabelle assured her.

At last, the front door swung open and Mom, Dad, and Matthew walked in. Matthew began chatting excitedly as soon as he saw his sisters. "After the zoo, we met Mom at the conference, and then we got—"

"That sounds great, but can we hear about this later?" Amanda blurted. "Mom, Dad, we have big, important news!" She told them about meeting Chris Savoie, and about how

Molly noticed that the autograph was actually evidence.

Amanda paused and looked at Molly, then cleared her throat. "And there's one other thing, too..." She told them about the scary note the twins had found in their room.

"So we *have* to go to the police now," Molly said quickly. "Don't you agree?"

Mom and Dad looked at each other for a moment. Then Mom nodded and Dad put his jacket back on. "I agree with you," he said. "The police need to hear about this."

"Why did you keep that note a secret, girls?" Mom said. "That could have been very dangerous! You should know better!"

Molly and Amanda nodded. "Sorry, Mom," Molly said. "We were afraid that you would make us go home early."

"Your safety is the most important thing. If something like this ever happens again, you must tell Dad and me right away," Mom said. "But hurry up now and get your jackets on. We need to go to the police station."

"We're going to the police station!" said Matthew. "This is awesome!"

Secretly, Molly and Amanda agreed with him.

"It's so cool to solve an actual mystery!" exclaimed Molly.

"And it's even better that it will help Alain and Marie," Amanda added.

chapter 14

"Now that the conference is over, I can finally relax!" Mom said the next morning.

"And now that the mystery is solved, *we* can finally relax!" Molly said, nudging her sister. Everyone had slept late that morning, after the excitement of the night before. Mom, Dad, Matthew, the twins, and Isabelle had met Chris at the police station. The twins and Chris told the police everything they knew, and Molly handed over the autograph. The police hadn't said much, but they were *very* interested in the twins' story.

Matthew was disappointed that the police weren't going to arrest Claude right then, but Chris promised to keep them updated. Now all they could do was wait to hear how the story ended.

After everyone had woken up, the twins and Matthew crowded into bed with Mom to watch TV. Dad had picked up two cafés au lait and three orange juices. "Barbara, want to go to the Court of Two Sisters for dinner tonight?" he asked Mom.

She smiled at him. "Sounds good to me," she replied.

"But what are we gonna do today?" Matthew asked.

"I was thinking we could take a riverboat ride on the

Mississippi River," Dad suggested. "It's not a swamp tour, but it's still pretty fun."

"Great idea," Mom agreed. "Now let's all get ready—we missed breakfast downstairs so we'll have to pick something up on the way."

"*Oooh,* can we get some of those delicious beignets?" Amanda asked excitedly.

An hour later, the Moores were relaxing on the deck of a big paddleboat that was slowly cruising on the Mississippi River. Amanda and Molly sat back on two deck chairs as the warm afternoon sun shone on their faces.

"This is wonderful," Amanda said with a happy sigh. The big paddle in the back of the boat made a soothing, rushing sound like a waterfall as it cut through the water. Matthew kept leaning out over the side to watch the water cascade as the paddle turned around and around. Just like on the swamp tour, he leaned over a little *too* far and Mom and Dad had to reach out to prevent him from falling!

"Be careful, sport!" Dad said with a laugh. "I think we've already had enough excitement for one family vacation!"

Afterward, the Moores hopped on a streetcar heading to St. Charles Avenue and their hotel. At Rivet Mansion, everyone changed for dinner. Amanda wore a pale blue skirt and top with her sparkly blue barrettes, and Molly wore her black pants and green peasant top again.

Amanda and Molly were amazed when they first saw the stately old restaurant at 613 Royal Street. They passed through a fancy iron gate to enter the restaurant's court-yard, which was filled with all kinds of plants, including banana trees and a weeping willow, and had a fountain in the center. The Court of Two Sisters seemed a world apart from the street around it. People sat around the court-yard and sipped drinks as a jazz band played.

"We couldn't leave without hearing a jazz band," said Mom. "After all, New Orleans is the home of jazz."

"Who were the two sisters?" Molly wanted to know.

Mom had picked up a brochure on the way in and was now looking it over. "It says they were two Creole sisters, Emma and Bertha Camors, who were born in New Orleans just before the Civil War. They ran a fancy shop, the Shop of the Two Sisters, right here. It says that although they were two years apart, they were as alike as twins."

Molly remembered the idea she'd had about owning a restaurant with Amanda someday. "Take our picture here, please," she asked Dad. She stood in front of a plaque that read "The Court of Two Sisters."

"That's us, all right," Amanda said. "Two sisters!" She

131

put her arm around Molly's shoulders and they tipped their heads toward each other and smiled. As the camera flashed, Molly imagined the picture hanging in the lobby of their restaurant one day.

Dad clapped his hands together. "I don't know about the rest of you, but I'm getting hungry. Let's go in!"

Inside the family was awed by the elegant surroundings and even more impressed when they were seated and the waiter handed them each a menu.

"Crawfish Louise," Mom read. "'Crawfish in a traditional Cajun blend of seasoning and spice.' That sounds delicious."

"I'm going to have the jambalaya," Dad announced.

Matthew's eyes widened with surprise. "Hey, they serve poison here!" he announced.

"That's not *poison*," Mom corrected him gently. "It's *poisson*. It means 'fish' in French."

"Well, I'm *not* eating it," Matthew insisted. "I want pasta. Just plain pasta."

"Pasta sounds good to me, too," Amanda said. "*Mmmm,* this Pasta La Lou looks yummy."

"Crawfish, shrimp, andouille sausage, and vegetables over pasta," Molly read from the menu. "Yeah, I want Pasta La Lou, too!"

The meal was so delicious that on the way out,

Amanda and Molly decided to buy the Court of Two Sisters cookbook for Dish.

"Now these two sisters can make all these delicious Creole dishes anytime we want!" Molly exclaimed.

"*And* it has a whole chapter of desserts!" said Amanda with a grin.

All of a sudden, it was Saturday—the Moores' last full day in New Orleans. The twins were glum at breakfast—they weren't looking forward to going home the next day. But then a big surprise instantly cheered them up.

Mom cleared her throat. "I got a phone call this morning," she said to the twins. "From Marie."

"What did she say?" Molly asked breathlessly. Even Isabelle was listening intently.

"Claude was arrested yesterday," Mom replied in a low voice. "Alain and Marie are shocked, of course. But they're very grateful to you girls. And to you, too, Isabelle. They've invited us to a special dinner tonight to thank us."

"Wow! The restaurant's reopening? That's awesome!" Amanda cheered.

"Not until next week," Mom said. "Tonight's dinner will be private—just for us, and Isabelle, and Chris. I think it sounds like the perfect way to end our trip!"

"Definitely!" Molly exclaimed. "I can't wait for tonight!"

"Well, in the meantime, how about a trip to Jazzland, the amusement park?" Dad suggested, his blue eyes twinkling.

That afternoon the family forgot about Claude and the police as they flew down spectacular roller coasters at the park. They went to a section of the park that recreated New Orleans's Mardi Gras celebration, and one where they got another taste of being on the bayou in Cajun country. That evening—carrying postcards, plastic drink cups, prizes, and caps reading "Jazzland"—they came back to the hotel having had one of the best days of their vacation.

That night, the Moores dressed once more for dinner and, for the last time, arrived at Château Savoie. Marie greeted them in the front hall. She'd changed from her chef's clothing and wore a lovely black dress covered in red velvet roses.

"Come in! Welcome!" Marie exclaimed, leading them to a round table where Chris and Isabelle were already seated. Alain, wearing a dark suit, joined them at the table. Shane, the waiter, brought everyone an appetizer of shrimp in a saffron cream sauce.

Molly and Amanda grinned at each other. This was going to be a feast they would never forget!

Before anyone started eating, Alain rose from the table and lifted his glass. "A toast to Molly, Amanda, Isabelle, and Chris—four determined detectives who have saved Château Savoie. Marie and I thank you from the bottom of our hearts."

Mom and Dad beamed at the girls, who blushed as everyone clinked their glasses.

"It's such a shame that you can't be here next week for our grand reopening," Marie said as they began to eat the delicious appetizer. "I hope that someday you girls will come back and cook with us again!"

"We'd love to!" the twins said at the same time.

The next morning, the alarm started screeching shrilly while it was still dark outside. Molly slapped at it repeatedly, but with her eyes closed, she kept missing it.

"*Molls*," Amanda moaned. "What is that noise? Make it stop."

"It's the alarm," Molly said, waking up a little. She rolled onto her side and swatted at the travel clock one more time. "Got it!"

"Good, now we can go back to sleep," Amanda sighed with relief. The Moores had stayed at Château Savoie until after eleven, eating and dancing and laughing for hours. After the meal, Molly, Amanda, and Isabelle had showed everyone how to do the Mamou jitterbug. The twins were having such a great time that they didn't want the night to end, but eventually it was time to say good-bye. They had exchanged e-mail addresses with the Savoies and Isabelle, though, and promised to keep in touch.

The phone rang and Amanda instinctively grabbed for it. "Wake up, sleepy heads!" Mom's voice sang out.

"Okay," Amanda sighed. "We're up." She staggered out of bed and tapped Molly's shoulder. "It's back-to-Brooklyn day. Get up, Molls."

"I can't believe we're really home," Molly said as she pulled her suitcase into the Moores' quiet living room several hours later. It seemed unreal to think that only a short time ago they'd been in a city so far away and so different from Brooklyn.

"It feels like we never left, but also like we were away for a long time," Amanda told Mom.

"It always seems that way to me, too, after a vacation," Mom agreed as she began opening the living room shutters allowing sunlight to flood in.

The phone rang. Amanda dropped the suitcase she'd been carrying and ran to grab it. "The Voodoo Queen of New Orleans speaking," she giggled.

"What? Is that—Do I—Amanda?"

Amanda could tell it was Peichi. "Hey, Peichi. It's Amanda. We just got in."

"I'm glad you guys are back! I want to hear *every-thing* about your trip. Can you come over? Natasha's already here!"

"I'll ask. Just a sec." Amanda asked Mom if she and Molly could go.

"Please?" Molly pleaded. "I can't wait to tell everybody about the trip and give them their presents."

"All right," Mom agreed, "but just for a couple of hours. You have school tomorrow."

Amanda got back on the living room phone and Molly ran to get on the extension in the kitchen. They told Peichi they could come over.

"Want me to call Shawn?" Amanda offered.

Peichi didn't answer right away. "Um, not just yet, okay? We'll call her a little later."

"What's going on?" Molly asked.

"We'll tell you when you get here," Peichi promised.

The twins were dying to know what was happening, so they grabbed their friends' gifts and dashed out the door. When they arrived at Peichi's house, Natasha and Peichi were sitting on the front steps, talking and laughing.

"If I go back to school and everyone is saying I had a date with Omar I'll just hide in my locker and refuse to come out," Peichi was saying to Natasha. She noticed the twins and jumped up.

"*Ohmigosh!* You're *finally* back! Yay! I missed you guys so much!" Peichi shrieked as she pounced on the twins to hug them. Natasha held back shyly, but she had a big smile on her face.

"We missed you, too!" Molly said, hugging Natasha and Peichi. "And Omar's not *that* bad," she teased Peichi.

"He's kind of cute, in his own way," Amanda said, laughing as she hugged her friends.

"Oh, please. It's *too* embarrassing!" Peichi insisted as

they went inside and upstairs to her bedroom.

Amanda handed Peichi a gift wrapped in red tissue paper. "Maybe this will cheer you up," she said. Peichi unwrapped a decorative black and red fan.

"It's not exactly like your Chinese fans, but it's from the French Quarter in New Orleans and we thought it would be a cool addition to your collection," Molly explained.

"It's gorgeous! I love it!" Peichi exclaimed.

Natasha's gift was a small lamp with a beaded shade. "It's purple!" she cried happily. "Thanks!"

"For your new room," Amanda told her.

"Oh, guess what?" Peichi asked. "We have a cooking job next weekend, if you guys want to take it. Mrs. Freeman called me yesterday since you were away— she needs two dinners. Sounds pretty easy."

"Great!" Molly and Amanda chorused. "Did you talk to Shawn about it?" Molly asked.

Natasha and Peichi looked at each other. "We will later this afternoon. We, um, didn't want Shawn to come over just yet because we wanted to talk to you guys about Elizabeth," Natasha said.

"How's she doing?" asked Molly.

"She's really nice," Natasha said. "It's not so bad, having Elizabeth and her aunt upstairs—it's, like, their own space, so sometimes I even forget they moved in. And my new room looks so cool—I can't wait for you guys to see it."

"What happened with the big cheerleader sleepover?" asked Amanda, raising her eyebrows.

Peichi and Natasha exchanged another look. "It was...it was bad," Peichi answered.

"Elizabeth came home *crying*," Natasha said. "It was a disaster."

"What happened?" repeated Amanda.

"Angie," Peichi said. "Angie happened."

The twins groaned.

"Elizabeth told me Angie spent the whole night being totally horrible," Natasha explained. "She kept leaving Elizabeth out, and when the lights were turned off, she started whispering mean things about Elizabeth. She made fun of her accent and her clothes, and she even said stuff about the fact that Elizabeth lives with her aunt instead of her parents. Elizabeth heard the whole thing and was humiliated. And no one stood up for her."

"Not even Shawn," Peichi added.

The girls shook their heads sadly. None of them could figure out what happened to Shawn when Angie was around.

"Angie's *so, so* mean," Natasha said. "And other kids are going to start thinking Shawn's mean, too, since she's Angie's friend. Elizabeth doesn't trust Shawn at all now, even though I tried to convince her that Shawn is really nice. Should we talk to Shawn or what? I don't know *what* to do."

For a moment no one spoke.

"We should wait," Molly finally suggested. "If things get worse we'll talk to Shawn about it. But I don't think we should talk to Shawn *too* soon, or she might take it the wrong way, you know? I mean, maybe Angie will lighten up on Elizabeth—she's friends with everyone else on the cheerleading team."

Maybe, Amanda thought. *But I doubt it.* She cleared her throat. "Well, let's call Shawn now, anyway. I don't want her to be upset that we didn't invite her." The other girls nodded, and Amanda reached for the phone. But as she dialed Shawn's phone number, she thought to herself, *Why am I so worried about Shawn's feelings? She barely thinks about anybody besides Angie these days.*

The next day at school, Amanda raced down the hall to see whether her name was on the cast list for the spring play.

And it was!

"*Yes!* I got a part!" Amanda exclaimed happily. "Miss Peacock! Woo-hoo!"

"Way to go!" Molly cheered her sister and gave her a high five.

Amanda squeezed Molly. "I am *sooo* excited!" she said.

"Me, too," Molly said. "The first softball game is this Saturday! I can't wait!"

"You'll be awesome, Molls," Amanda said. "But we'd better save Sunday for the Freeman cooking job. What do you think we should make? Maybe something from our Court of Two Sisters cookbook?"

"Yeah! Or maybe alligator cheesecake!" said Molly as the twins hurried off to homeroom.

"I don't think our clients are ready for *that!*" Amanda said, laughing.

"Okay, but seriously, Manda, what do you think we should make?" Molly asked.

"Let's have a Dish meeting tomorrow after school," Amanda whispered as they slid into their seats just before the bell rang. Molly nodded.

It's gonna be awesome to cook for Dish again! Molly thought as the homeroom teacher, Mr. Flint, began taking attendance. The New Orleans vacation had been even better than she'd expected. Exploring Cypress Swamp and the French Quarter, meeting Isabelle and Madame Rivet, eating in amazing restaurants, cooking with Chef Alain and Marie, solving the Château Savoie mystery...Molly smiled as she remembered her trip.

She started to make a list of possible dishes to cook for Mrs. Freeman, thinking, *Vacation is over—it's time to get back to business!*

dish

The Amazing cookbook

By

The CHEF Girls

AMANDA!

Molly!

Peichi ☺

shawn!

Natasha!

Crawfish Louise

this is a traditional Cajun dish. the sauce is rich and delicious! When Mom ordered it at the Court of two Sisters, it was served over rice.

2 tablespoons olive oil
3 tablespoons margarine
2 cups sliced mushrooms
1 pound crawfish (or medium sized shrimp, peeled and deveined— that means to cut out the shrimp's gray vein. Have an adult do this for you!)

1/4 cup chopped green onion
1/2 cup water
1/2 tablespoon Italian seasoning
1 clove garlic, peeled and crushed
1/2 cup grated Parmesan cheese
1/4 cup chopped parsley
1/4 teaspoon black pepper
1 1/2 cups bread crumbs
1/4 teaspoon salt

1. Preheat the oven to 350 degrees.

2. Heat the olive oil and margarine together in a large, deep skillet over medium heat. Add the mushrooms, crawfish (or shrimp), and green onion. Cook for three minutes.

3. Add the water and continue cooking over medium heat, stirring the mixture every thirty seconds or so.

4. When the mixture is bubbling, add the Italian seasoning, garlic, Parmesan cheese, and parsley. Cook for three more minutes.

5. Turn off the heat and stir in the black pepper, bread crumbs, and salt.

6. Carefully pour everything from the skillet into a large casserole dish. Bake for ten minutes. Now your Crawfish Louise is done!

It's really good served over rice with vegetables on the side!

—Molly

PASTA LA LOU

MOLLS AND I LOVE PASTA, SO WE HAD THIS DISH AT THE
COURT OF TWO SISTERS. IT WAS GREAT! THERE ARE SO MANY
INTERESTING FLAVORS MIXED TOGETHER.

1/2 POUND BUTTER

1/2 POUND ANDOUILLE SAUSAGE

(OR YOU CAN USE SMOKED SAUSAGE)

1/2 POUND MEDIUM-SIZED SHRIMP

1/2 POUND MEDIUM-SIZED SHRIMP

(PEELED AND DEVEINED—HAVE AN ADULT DO THIS!)

1/2 POUND CRAWFISH TAILS (IF YOU DON'T HAVE CRAWFISH,

USE 1 POUND OF SHRIMP INSTEAD OF 1/2 POUND)

2 TABLESPOONS MINCED GARLIC

1 1/2 CUPS SLICED JUMBO MUSHROOMS

1/4 CUP DICED GREEN BELL PEPPER

1/4 CUP DICED RED BELL PEPPER

1/4 CUP CHOPPED GREEN ONIONS

1/2 TABLESPOON CREOLE SEASONING (YOU CAN GET THIS AT

THE SUPERMARKET—WE USE TONY CHACHERE'S OR ZATARAIN'S)

1 1/2 CUPS WATER

6 TABLESPOONS CORNSTARCH (DISSOLVED IN A LITTLE WATER)

1 POUND VERMICELLI PASTA, COOKED

1. MELT THE BUTTER IN A LARGE SKILLET. ADD THE SAUSAGE, CRAWFISH TAILS, SHRIMP, GARLIC, MUSHROOMS, PEPPERS, AND ONION. SAUTÉ UNTIL THE SAUSAGE IS SLIGHTLY BROWNED AND EVERYTHING IS COATED WITH THE MELTED BUTTER.

2. ADD THE WATER. WHEN THE MIXTURE IS SIMMERING, ADD THE CREOLE SEASONING. BRING TO A BOIL.

3. ONCE THE MIXTURE IS BOILING, ADD THE CORNSTARCH (DON'T FORGET TO DISSOLVE IT IN WATER FIRST!). THIS WILL HELP THICKEN THE SAUCE. REDUCE THE HEAT TO LOW AND STIR FOR TEN MORE MINUTES.

4. SERVE OVER THE COOKED VERMICELLI.

YUMMY!

PECAN PIE

THIS WAS MY FAVORITE DESSERT AT THE COURT OF TWO SISTERS! I WAS TOTALLY PSYCHED WHEN I SAW IT WAS INCLUDED IN THE COOKBOOK! IT'S SOOOO YUMMY, I KNOW YOU WILL LOVE IT, TOO. THE BEST PART IS THAT THIS RECIPE MAKES TWO PIES—SO YOU CAN GIVE ONE TO A FRIEND AND KEEP ONE FOR YOURSELF!

3 CUPS SHELLED PECANS
2 PASTRY PIE SHELLS
1 3/4 CUPS DARK CORN SYRUP
2 1/4 CUPS SUGAR

6 EGGS
1 1/2 TEASPOONS SALT
4 TABLESPOONS VANILLA EXTRACT
1/2 CUP BUTTER

1. PREHEAT THE OVEN TO 325 DEGREES. PLACE 1 1/2 CUPS EACH OF THE SHELLED PECANS IN THE PIE SHELLS AND BAKE FOR FIVE MINUTES. THIS WILL TOAST THE PECANS AND MAKE THEM REALLY YUMMY!

2. WHILE YOU'RE WAITING, SEPARATE THE EGG WHITES FROM THE YOLKS. IF YOU HAVEN'T DONE THIS BEFORE, HAVE AN ADULT SHOW YOU HOW! THROW OUT THE YOLKS.

3. TAKE THE PIE SHELLS OUT OF THE OVEN AND SET ASIDE. IN A LARGE MIXING BOWL, COMBINE THE CORN SYRUP AND SUGAR. CREAM IN THE EGG WHITES, BUTTER, SALT, AND VANILLA EXTRACT. MIX ON LOW SPEED FOR FIVE MINUTES. THIS IS THE FILLING MIXTURE!

4. POUR 2 1/2 CUPS OF THE FILLING MIXTURE OVER THE TOASTED PECANS IN EACH PIE SHELL. BAKE THE PIES AT 325 DEGREES FOR FORTY MINUTES, OR UNTIL THE CENTER OF EACH PIE IS FIRM WHEN TOUCHED LIGHTLY WITH A FORK OR KNIFE. MMMMM!

cooking tips from the chef girls!

The Chef Girls are looking out for you!
Here are some things you should
know if you want to cook.
(Remember to ask your parents
if you can use knives and the stove!)

1 Tie back long hair so that it won't
   get into the food or in the way as
   you work.

2 Don't wear loose-fitting clothing
   that could drag in the food or
   on the stove burners.

3 Never cook in bare feet or open-toed
   shoes. Something sharp or hot could
   drop on your feet.

4 Always wash your hands before you
   handle food.

5   Read through the recipe before you start. Gather your ingredients together and measure them before you begin.

6   Turn pot handles in so that they won't get knocked off the stove.

7   Use wooden spoons to stir hot liquids. Metal spoons can become very hot.

8   When cutting or peeling food, cut away from your hands.

9   Cut food on a cutting board, not the countertop.

10   Hand someone a knife with the knifepoint pointing to the floor.

11   Clean up as you go. It's safer and neater.

12   Always use a dry pot holder to remove something hot from the oven. You could get burned with a wet one, since wet ones retain heat.

13   Make sure that any spills on the floor are cleaned up right away, so that you don't slip and fall.

14 Don't put knives in clean-up water. You could reach into the water and cut yourself.

15 Use a wire rack to cool hot baking dishes to avoid scorch marks on the countertop.

An Important Message from the Chef Girls!

Some foods can carry bacteria, such as salmonella, that can make you sick.
To avoid salmonella, always cook poultry, ground beef, and eggs thoroughly before eating.
Don't eat or drink foods containing raw eggs.
And wash hands, kitchen work surfaces, and utensils with soap and water immediately after they have been in contact with raw meat or poultry.

mooretimes2: Molly and Amanda

qtpie490: Shawn

happyface: Peichi

BrooklynNatasha: Natasha

JustMac: Justin

Wuzzup: What's up?

Mwa smooching sound

G2G: Got To Go

deets: details

b-b: Bye-Bye

brb: be right back

<3 hearts

L8R: Later, as in "See ya later!"

LOL: Laughing Out Loud

GMTA: Great Minds Think Alike

j/k: Just kidding

B/C: because

W8: Wait

W8 4 me @: Wait for me at

thanx: thanks

BK: Big kiss

MAY: Mad about you

RUF2T?: Are you free to talk?

TTUL: Type to you later

E-ya: will e-mail you

LMK: Let me know

GR8: Great

WFM: Works for me

2: to, too, two

C: see

u: you

2morrow: tomorrow

VH: virtual hug

BFFL: Best Friends For Life

:-@ shock

:-P sticking out tongue

%-) confused

:-o surprised

;-) winking or teasing